Quests

Guardians Of The Forest Book 2

What people have said ...

...book two of this magical trilogy continues the story and takes the reader deeper into the Forest and deeper into the danger faced by its people, the Danae. It is just as gripping as the first book. By now the characters have become old friends and it is exciting to follow them as they continue their adventures. This time they have to call on even greater powers of strength and daring as they set out to find the legendary Sleih, whose help they need. But first they must find out whether the Sleih actually exist or are simply an echo of old folk memory. If you've read the first book, you'll definitely want to continue with this one.

...the adventure continues with new locations and characters introduced. Finished this one within 24 hours ... very engaging.

Also by the author

The Wild army Guardians Of The Forest Book 1

Gryphon Magic Guardians Of The Forest Book 3

www.cherylburman.com

First published in the UK in 2020 by Holborn House Ltd

Prologue

The line of laden wagons rumbled south. Stoves and pots, chairs and tables and cages with chickens and ducks swayed from side to side. Crying children clung to piles of bedding. Lowing cows and bleating sheep crowded the road. Red dust rose and fell again to settle on bare arms and hats and the backs of the sturdy horses hauling the Danae and all the worldly goods they could carry, bearing them away from their homes.

'Go into the Deep Forest,' the Madach had commanded. 'Go into the Deep Forest of Arneithe and find new homes.'

The bleating of the goats tethered behind the wagons mixed with the children's complaints until Josh was unsure which was which. He cradled his baby sister in his arms.

Little Clara, sweet baby.

Already she laughed when Josh pulled faces at her or danced a silly dance. With her silken black hair and golden skin, Clara was the one of all Josh's brothers and sisters who most bore the look of their Sleih great-great-grandmamma. Which is why it was Clara who wore around her chubby neck the silver chain with the tiny jewelled gryphon pendant.

A magic charm, family lore said. Wards off evil, Josh's mother said. It was her Sleih great-grandmamma who first owned the pendant, although how she came to own it, no one knew.

Josh wasn't convinced by the jewel. It hadn't stopped the

Madach from driving his family from their home, had it?

The trail of wagons shuddered to a ragged halt. Josh wondered why. It was too early on this summer day to camp for the night. And then Josh saw them.

Sleih riders on black horses, filling the road ahead.

The Danae quieted. The cows and the sheep and the goats quieted too, no doubt at the behest of the Sleih riders.

The old king was among them. He was speaking, but Josh was too far away to hear the speech and too young to hear the words through his mind, as many of the older Danae could. What he did hear was a murmuring among the Danae and a stirring like wind through ripe wheat. When the murmuring had passed, his mother lifted Clara from Josh's arms and hugged the baby close to her chest.

Josh watched, with an uneasy sense of loss settling in his stomach. He was startled when a lady of the Sleih, a Seer, appeared beside the wagon.

The Seer held out her arms and Josh's mother gently placed Clara into them. The Seer gazed down at the baby and smiled with a tenderness Josh had not known the Sleih could achieve.

Clara seemed content.

But then the Seer's smile turned thin-lipped and her golden brow furrowed. With one hand she undid the clasp of the gryphon pendant and held it, gingerly, as if it might scorch her. She pressed it into Josh's mother's hand.

'This should not reside in Ilatias,' the Seer said.

Josh's mother held the jewel to her wet cheek.

'To remember her by,' she said.

'To remember her by,' the Seer acknowledged, and rode north, joining other Sleih lords and ladies riding back to Ilatias.

Josh saw that each one carried before them a Danae babe.

Chapter One

A Boar And A Bear

Boom!

The thunderous shock drowned out for a heartbeat the shrieking of the wind. Mark jumped. He drew his cloak tighter about his shivering body. A vision of far away home brought self-pitying tears to his already wet eyes.

'We have to get out of this!'

'Where?' Gwen's voice sounded thin, pitched against the hammering rain. 'I can't see anything, it's too dark.'

Lightning lit the gnarled trees.

Mark jolted backwards.

What was that?

Gwen screamed. She clutched Mark's arm.

'A bear! It's a bear! Run!'

Another flash lit the trees. A monstrous black shape reared above Mark. Its roar matched the thunder.

Mark's throat went dry. He jerked the arm Gwen grasped. 'Run, Gwen, run!'

The dark came down, darker than before the lightning.

Something heavy and moving fast brushed past Mark.

More bears? His terror grew.

Whatever it was butted him hard. He grabbed at Gwen, pulling her with him, into the mud.

An unearthly squealing added to Gwen's screams and to the crash of the thunder and the roaring of the bear.

Mark spluttered, trying to stand, to run. Gwen floundered beside him.

The squealing went on, and on, pitched high against the deep bellow of the bear.

Mark lurched to his feet.

Lightning, a short flash, enough for Mark to glimpse the biggest boar he'd ever seen. The creature struggled with the bear, long tusks impaled in the dark fur, its hind legs thrust into the muddy earth. The bear howled, twisting its body to shake the boar free.

Darkness.

The uproar from the bear and the boar challenged the boom of thunder and the screech of the wind.

Mark tugged at Gwen's cloak. 'Come on!'

They clung to each other, stumbling through the slippery wetness. Thin branches slapped at Mark's face and tore at his clothes. Stones and roots grabbed his feet.

Shelter. They needed shelter.

Mark squinted through the rain. His breath came in spasms. His cloak wrapped its sodden wetness around his legs. Any moment, he would fall where he was.

'There!' He pointed to a darker gap between the trees. 'It might be a cave.'

Gwen ran towards the darkness, squelching through unseen puddles. Mark splashed beside her. Water seeped through his cracked boots, soaking his chilled feet. Flashes of lightning lit their way.

Gwen stopped in front of an ivy-covered gash in the rock. 'Might be more bears.' She shivered. 'Or wolves.'

Mark gulped deep breaths. They had to get out of the storm. He pushed through the ivy to lean into the cave. No smell of wild animals. He poked a leg through the gap, listening. Nothing, except his own heart thudding in his ears.

'It's safe.'

Gwen fell through the ivy behind him, into the dryness and quiet. And the pitch blackness. Mark heard the soft thump as Gwen slumped to the ground. He dropped beside her, his wet cloak bunched at his back. He could smell the dankness of last year's leaves on his hair and clothes.

Gwen let out a shuddering sigh. 'What ... happened?'

'A boar ... a boar, huge! It pushed me over.'

'It saved us ... didn't it? From ... the bear.'

'Saved us? You think it meant to save us?' Mark found the idea startling.

'No.' Gwen noisily sucked in air. 'It wanted the bear. We were in its way.' She let out a deep breath. 'I suppose.'

Beyond the curtain of ivy, the clatter of the rain had quietened and the thunder and lightning had moved on through the Deep Forest. The wind's squalling turned fitful, as if it too was tired of the storm and wanted to rest.

'Listen,' Gwen said.

'What?'

'There's a noise, not the wind, something else. Do you hear it?'

Mark strained to hear. There it was, above the faltering wind. A wild howl, answered by another, and another.

'Wolves,' Gwen said. 'Again.'

The cries of wolves had followed them for many days, the fearsome noise seeming closer each night. Every evening, Mark made sure the fire blazed hotly bright, waking from time to time to keep the flames glowing. He and Gwen slept close together, as near to the blaze as they dared.

'It's too dark to see if there's anything to light a fire with,' Mark said.

'Let's hope the wolves stay at home tonight, out of this storm.'

Mark heard the tiredness in Gwen's voice. He shivered and rubbed his hands together. 'Isn't it summer? Isn't it supposed to be warm? And not rain as much?' He wanted to distract them both from frightening visions of wolves and bears. And wild boar big enough to attack bears.

'We have storms like this at home in the summer, too, remember?'

'Home.' Mark sighed. 'It's been forever since we left home.'

'Yes. And still no clue if we're getting closer to these Sleih. It's all well and good to say the Sleih are in the west, if anyone knew how far west.'

'Assuming there are Sleih.'

It was a conversation he and Gwen had every day while they traipsed along narrow animal trails which more often than not ended at a prickly holly or a stand of nettles or a stony cliff edge. Trying to keep west, they'd splashed across countless streams, slipped and slithered on mossy stones, scrambled up steep banks and pushed their way through scrub-filled valleys.

The forest itself seemed to not want to help. It wasn't like their own friendly Forest with playful streams and trees which stayed in the same place year in and year out. The deeper they wandered into this forest, the deeper the darkness below the ancient trees, the fewer trails there were – and the more of them which led nowhere – and the stranger the night grunts and whistles and whispers which disturbed their unquiet rest. They had camped beside tall leafy beech trees to wake the next morning under a willow, or an ash tree. Had the trees moved? Had they themselves been moved?

Mark had seen Gwen's strained, unbelieving face and known his own was the same. The creeping chill of feeling constantly watched never left him.

Then the wolves started their nightly howling. And now there were bears and giant boar to worry about.

And they still didn't know if there were any Sleih to be found.

'I don't think we'll ever reach these Sleih,' Mark said, as he did every day. 'I think they're a fairytale. And if they are real, and if we find them, why would they want to help us?'

Mark heard Gwen shifting on the dry floor.

'I don't know,' she said. 'I only know we promised Ma we'd bring back an army of Sleih and we have to keep on until we either reach the Sleih or find out they don't exist.'

'And Lucy, too,' Mark said. 'We've got to try and find Lucy.'

In the dark cave, wet and cold, the task was overwhelming. He lay down, wriggling to find a spot where a stone didn't jab into him, pushing a damp bag into place to serve as a pillow. 'What I wouldn't give to hear Ma yelling at me to hurry up with the firewood before the stove went out.'

'I know.' Gwen sighed. 'And Callie carrying on about the animals.' She paused. 'Callie, the animals ...'

'What about Callie and her animals?'

'Nothing, not really. It's what she said about the wild creatures helping us. Why would she say that?'

Mark grunted. Callie was strange, that was all he knew.

The sound of Gwen pummelling her own pillow-bag reached him. 'Let's try and sleep, see what the morning brings.'

Chapter Two

The Caverns

'Stop kicking me,' Mark grumbled in his sleep.

'I'm not.'

Mark forced open an eye. A stout leg covered in dark scratched leather filled his view. It wasn't Gwen's leg.

'What?' He jumped up, got tangled in his damp cloak, and ended on his back.

A band of yellow sun had found its way around the curtain of ivy. By its light Mark saw Gwen, her hands clenched at her sides, staring at a man with a brown beard.

It wasn't just one bearded face. Two others peered down at Mark. One beard was blonde and curly, the other grey, scattered with the last vestiges of black hairs struggling to keep their place.

'You're Danae!' Gwen said, at the same time the brown-bearded man said, 'What are you doing here?'

The strangers were dressed in leather and furs. Otherwise they looked much the same as the villagers at home with their creamy skin, tinged by the merest hint of golden honey, and their stocky frames.

'Danae?' Greybeard shook his head. 'No, we're not Danae. We do know of the Danae of old, of course.'

'Who are you?' Brownbeard said.

'We're Danae, from the Forest, by the sea,' Gwen said, 'and we're looking for the Sleih, if the Sleih exist, because we need their help.'

'Sleih?' Greybeard raised his eyebrows.

'Better come with us,' the man with the brown beard said, and walked to the back of the cave.

Mark gazed after him. The daylight showed their shelter from the storm was a large cavern. Its high rocky walls ran deep into the darkness of the hillside where all three men were heading.

'What do you think? Should we go?' he said.

'What do I think?' Gwen crossed her arms. 'About going with strangers into the depths of the earth?' If the men could hear her, they paid no attention. 'I think it's stupid.'

'They seem harmless enough.' Mark watched as the first of the men disappeared into the blackness. 'They sound like they know something about the Sleih. I think we should go.'

'Go? Where? And who are they if they're not Danae?'

Mark shrugged. The second man moved out of sight.

'Do you have any better ideas?'

The third man reached the darkness at the end of the cavern. Mark shook Gwen's arm.

'We've been wandering this forest for weeks and we're no closer to finding these Sleih. If they can be found at all.'

'They could be anyone! It could be dangerous.'

'They might have Lucy.'

Gwen blinked and Mark threw in one last argument. 'Whatever happens, it's got to be better than being eaten by bears.'

He picked up his muddy, loosely rolled blanket and his bags, threw his cloak over his shoulders and walked after the bearded men. He didn't look back.

Behind him, Gwen muttered, 'This is stupid.'

Mark glanced around to see her hesitate a moment longer before picking up her own blanket, bags and cloak and hurrying after him.

The men had disappeared to the left. A light flared, and as Mark rounded the corner he saw each man held a glowing lantern.

Gwen caught up to him. 'This had better be all right.'

'Come along,' the grey-bearded man said.

He ushered them into the space behind the first man, and off they went, tramping steadily and silently through the musty tunnels. In the wavering light from the lanterns, Mark had to concentrate on the stony path. The rocky walls closed in tight and the roof was low enough in places to force him to stoop. The lantern-bearers went left, right, ignored many tunnels, paused at junctions where they inspected both ways before carrying on down one or other passage. They saw no one else. Occasionally the echoes of distant banging rang through the tunnels. The blackness beyond their hosts' lanterns was complete.

They'd never find their way out by themselves, Mark realised. A nervous flutter tickled his throat. Hopefully nothing unpleasant waited for them at the end of this journey. Hopefully, news of the Sleih, or even the Sleih themselves, waited for them. Then Gwen would be sorry she'd hesitated. He looked over his shoulder. Gwen's face was white. Beads of sweat stood out on her forehead. Her eyes were fixed on the stony ground.

'Are you all right?'

Gwen's eyes flickered to the low ceiling. 'Do you think it's safe?'

'Seems solid to me. See, the roof's higher here and I think the tunnel's wider.'

Gwen lifted her head and puffed out a small breath. They marched on, Mark grateful to be able to stand upright. The roof rose higher. Gwen's face regained its colour and the beads of sweat dried. From time to time she shot Mark a furious look.

At last they came to passages poorly lit by smoky flames from lanterns set far apart on the rock walls. Their escorts darkened their own lamps. More people dressed in skins and furs appeared in the passages to trail behind the silent group.

How sombre these cave dwellers were, Mark thought. He supposed if he lived underground he might be sombre too.

'Hi, Maikin, who are these?' a man said. 'Where did you find them?'

Maikin, the one with the brown beard, didn't break stride. 'Can't talk, busy.'

They passed caves as dully lit as the tunnels. Animal skins or dry grass patchily covered the floors. The smell of cooking meat rose from pots suspended over small fires. Men, women and children sat in smoky silence at roughly made tables, eating or preparing food, or simply sitting.

There was no laughter, no voices raised in argument. Mark wanted to shout, to break the sullen quiet.

'It's an underground village,' he said to Gwen, who was also peeking into the caves. 'A quiet village.'

'Wouldn't suit me.' Gwen lifted her eyes briefly to the shadowed roof.

'Here we are,' Maikin said. 'Wait here.'

His two companions darted ahead to a pair of arched and studded wooden doors. One of the doors opened a crack to let them slip inside.

A tremor of excitement ran through Mark's belly.

Were the Sleih behind those doors? Was their endless wandering over?

Chapter Three

The Queen And The Truthteller

To take her mind off the weight of rock and earth above her, Gwen imagined what was behind the heavy wooden doors. Likely they led into a hall, like the Elders' grand hall at home. It wouldn't be filled with ornate wooden carvings like the Elders' hall. It would be decorated with gleaming precious stones and the floor would be strewn with sweet-smelling dried grasses or covered with deep, soft pelts. The whole space would glow with the light of numerous lanterns around its high, smooth walls, the roof so far distant she wouldn't notice she was underground.

Was this where they would discover if the Sleih were real and how to find them? Or maybe – she thrilled at the thought – the Sleih themselves were behind the doors.

The door opened.

'Come along,' Maikin said. He led Mark and Gwen through the slim opening. The door shut behind them with a soft thud.

Gwen's shoulders slumped. More gloom. A cavern the size of a big room, its rocky roof low and shadowed. A scattering of smouldering torches gave out spots of flickering yellow light. Rough rock walls were adorned only with long licks of moss-green water seeping through from the earth above.

Silent groups of people eyed the new arrivals. Gwen returned their morose scrutiny. They appeared to be simply more Danae, like Maikin and his bearded friends. Like the people she'd seen in the dim passageways and caves.

Maikin prodded Gwen and Mark across the bare earth floor.

'Majesty, may I present these strangers to you, found Above Ground this morning,' he said. 'They seek the Sleih.'

Gwen stared. Majesty? This was what queens were like?

Her Majesty's wispy, greying hair was untidily piled on top of her head, crushed beneath a dull beaten-metal crown sparsely decorated with ordinary stones. Her face was white, as if she never saw the sun. Her eyes could have been any colour, the irises overtaken by hugely dilated pupils which drank in all the light they could find. Her lips were thin and as white as her face.

Her Majesty eased forward to better examine Gwen and Mark. Her black leather dress strained against her bulky body.

'Are you spies?' she hissed.

Gwen stepped back and bumped into Maikin. 'No, we're Danae, like you,' she said. She was mesmerised by those black pupils.

The queen drew herself upright. 'We are not Danae. We are Sleih.'

'Sleih?' Mark said. 'You're the Sleih?'

Gwen's eyes widened. These people were the Sleih? She and Mark had found them? They had reached the end of searching?

She waited to feel happy, relieved, delighted.

Nothing.

She took in the gloomy cavern, the grey and white queen and the sullen people. Really? These were the mythical, fairytale Sleih? Gwen struggled with her disappointment. Had the Sleih fallen on bad times? Had the Madach driven them from their lands too?

'Yes, Sleih.' The queen's black eyes darted from Mark to Gwen. 'The protectors of the Danae.'

'Are there Danae here as well?' Gwen said at the same time Mark said, 'Is Lucy here?'

The queen's forehead creased.

'Our sister, who disappeared into the Forest,' Mark said. 'We hoped she was with the Sleih.'

The queen waved her hand. 'No, no Lucy, no Danae, not here, not for many, many years.'

Gwen had a new reason for disappointment and this one lay heavier in her stomach. Her mother had been wrong.

The queen was telling Maikin, 'You have done well, Maikin, to bring us Danae to protect, as is ever our duty.'

Maikin bowed. 'Thank you, Majesty.'

The queen inclined her head. The dull metal crown slipped sideways. She pushed it back in place, holding her neck stiffly to stop the crown slipping again.

'If you are not spies, why do you seek the Sleih?' she said.

Gwen held on to the thought these Sleih thought of themselves as protectors of the Danae. She must make her plea and see what happened.

'Our people live at the edge of the Forest,' she said, 'by the sea. Madach have come and we're afraid they'll drive us away like they drove us from The Place Before.'

The queen absently pushed her sliding crown back into place.

'The legends say the Sleih helped us then,' Mark said, 'so we thought they – you – might help us this time too, if they're – you're – not a myth, which everyone thinks they are.'

'A myth? Of course not. Why, here we are, in front of you. Of course we're not a myth.' The queen scowled at Mark before turning to Gwen. 'What do you want from us?'

'Majesty, we hoped you might have soldiers to help us fight these Madach, push them into the sea, send them back to wherever they came from.'

The queen leaned back in her throne. 'We will need to think on this.'

'Majesty'–Maikin coughed to attract the queen's attention–

'Majesty, we don't have an army. I can't see how we can help these Danae in the Forest.'

Gwen flashed him a quick glance. No soldiers? No help? The heavy disappointment in her stomach plunged to her soul.

'This is true. There may be other ways to help.' The queen closed her eyes, as if considering the other ways.

Gwen fought for hope. If there were other ways, maybe, just maybe, the bears and wolves and being lost in a forest of shifting trees and unseen eyes, wouldn't have all been for nothing.

'For the time being,' the queen said, snapping open her black eyes, 'you must stay here, with us. You must keep safe from these dangerous Madach. If you stay with us, we can protect you.'

Gwen started to say, 'Thank you,' but the queen wasn't listening. Her black stare had shifted sharply to where a high, thin voice sang out from across the cavern.

'Danae, the Danae of the Forest, where the monster threatens, the hissing monster, biting the trees ...'

A girl of about her own age walked steadily towards Gwen. The girl held her slim white arms out in front of her. Her hair hung straight down her back to her waist, smooth and black. Her deep green eyes stared, unseeing.

The Sleih murmured. The queen sat, unmoving, on her cold throne.

Maikin tugged at Gwen's arm. 'Come on. You mustn't listen to her. She makes no sense.'

Gwen resisted, watching the girl approach. The green eyes drew her. They could have been Callie's eyes.

'... the animals flee, they die ... their fear sears her mind ... oh ...' The girl held her head in her hands as if she was in pain. 'The market sellers call ... a fairytale my lord, a fairytale ...'

Gwen started. Fairytale! Like in Callie's nightmares.

The girl's hands dropped to her sides. She faced Gwen with

18

blank eyes. 'You must seek the Sleih, you must journey to the Sleih, for there lies help.'

The queen clutched the arms of her throne and glared at the girl. At the mention of the Sleih, she bent forward, her chins trembling. The others in the room ceased their whispering, intent on the girl, and on the queen.

Silence hung in the cavern like a fog.

Gwen frowned. Journey to the Sleih? Hadn't they found the Sleih?

Mark said it aloud. 'Aren't you the Sleih?'

The queen's knuckles whitened on the arms of her stone throne.

The girl's high voice echoed through the cave. 'Where is the Guardian of the Forest? Why has the Guardian failed? Ill? Dying? She has gone.'

She stretched out an arm to touch Gwen's cheek. Her eyelids fluttered, her white face suffused with red, and she dropped her arm. 'Oh, sorry, sorry.'

Gwen took the girl's cool hand in her own. 'What do you mean? Haven't we found the Sleih?'

'What monster?' Mark said. 'What's the guardian? We don't have a guardian, or a queen. We have a senior Elder.'

Maikin slid between the girl and Gwen, forcing Gwen to let go of the girl's hand.

'Don't pay her any mind,' he said. 'Mad she is, like her mother and her mother's mother, back to when no one can remember. All mad.'

Gwen leaned around Maikin. 'What's your name?'

'Verian. Truthteller.'

The queen snorted in an un-queenly manner. 'Truthteller, indeed. All lies and fantasies. Mad, just as Maikin says.'

Verian bowed her head. Gwen saw she was shaking.

The queen awkwardly shifted forward. 'I have said we need to think on the Danae request.' Her black eyes swivelled to

19

Maikin. 'Take them away. Feed them if they need feeding, bathe them if they need bathing, let them sleep if they need sleep. And when we have deliberated, we will summon them to hear our decision.'

She shoo'd Gwen and Mark from the room. She ignored Verian.

Maikin put his hand on Gwen's back to steer her to the wooden doors, opened one a crack and nudged her through. Gwen glanced back at Verian.

She stood, head bowed, before the strange queen's throne.

Chapter Four

Mad Women

'Do you think we've done it, reached the Sleih?' Mark said, spooning up his bowl of stew.

The stew had been brought by a young boy who kept his head down as he set the food out before silently scurrying off. It was good stew, herb-flavoured, full of a meat Gwen didn't recognise and didn't want to ask about. It was the first hot food she and Mark had eaten for many days.

'So they tell us, and I suppose there's no reason why the Sleih shouldn't look like the Danae.' Gwen scraped the sides of the dish with a bent metal spoon and pushed it aside. 'I did think they'd be more, well, romantic, you know?'

'Romantic? Like noble kings and queens with golden crowns riding fine horses? Like in the old stories?'

'Yes, I suppose.'

Gwen gazed around the small cave which Maikin had led them to. Feather-filled leather mattresses smothered in furs took up one side of the stony floor. On the opposite side, a slow trickle of strange-smelling, warm water forever filled a narrow basin cut into the rock wall before overflowing into an open drain. A wooden barrel next to the drain held cold, fresh water. There was the wooden table and its two chairs, a few crude bowls and utensils. Nothing else.

It was luxury for Gwen after weeks in the Deep Forest, despite being underground. Warm water to wash the grime and sweat from her face! She'd scrubbed until her skin tingled. Mattresses, and furs to sleep under! Still, it was hardly the stuff of mythical kings and queens. For a while Gwen contemplated the reality of the grey and white queen with her dull metal crown and no army. She sighed, and picked up her empty bowl.

'What the girl, Verian, said, frightens me,' she said. 'Monsters biting the trees, animals dying. Sounds too much like Callie's nightmares.'

And the girl and Callie shared the same deep green eyes, if that meant anything.

'What did she mean about a guardian? And fairytales?' Gwen set the bowl in a basin by the wooden barrel. 'If this Sleih queen won't help us, we'll have to find our way home, see what's happening.'

'What about Lucy? We have to find Lucy as well.'

'I wish I knew how.'

Mark fidgeted in his chair. 'Do you think we could go and explore while we wait?'

'Yes, we should.' Gwen pushed back her too long fringe. 'I'd feel much better if we knew the way out of here, just in case. And we should find Verian, see if we can't make sense of what she said. Especially about the Sleih.'

Mark was already at the cave opening. He peered up and down the long passage. 'Which way?'

When Gwen shrugged, he shrugged back and set off to the left.

The caves' cheerless silent dwellers hurried or strolled along passages where the stony floors were worn smooth from long years of traffic. Occasionally someone gave Mark and Gwen a curious glance. Nobody greeted them.

As they passed another barely lit cave, Gwen put her hand out to stop Mark.

'Verian?' she said.

At the sound of her name, Verian's head came up sharply.

She ran to Gwen and Mark. 'You shouldn't be here. Come in, quickly, before anyone sees.'

She no longer stared as if unseeing, although her unsmiling face made Gwen wonder if she and Mark were welcome here. Verian didn't hesitate however. She pulled Gwen into the room, at the same time loosening a heavy curtain to cover the entry.

'Why shouldn't we be here?' Mark said.

'Because they worry what nonsense we might tell you.'

This new voice came from a bundle of patchy furs at the far side of the cave. A small fire burned nearby, a kettle suspended over its red embers. White smoke rose from the fire in a thin stream to escape through a narrow opening in the low roof. A woman rested against scuffed leather pillows, her face set in a welcoming smile which deepened the tired creases around her eyes.

'Mama, you must not tire yourself.' Verian crouched down by her mother, gazing up at Gwen and Mark. 'She is gravely ill. There is no more we can do, except wait.'

There was no doubting these two were mother and daughter. Both had the same long, black hair – the mother's streaked with grey – and the same deep, sea-green eyes, a little too large for their delicate, pale faces. The mother's slim hands, blue veins showing through the translucent white skin, grasped the edge of a thinning fur cover.

'I'm sorry,' Gwen said. 'We should go.'

'No, no, please don't,' the mother said. 'Verian has told me about you, and your quest for the Sleih.' She gave a deep, wheezing cough. 'I was going to send her in search of you. There are things you should know before our queen summons you.'

This speech left her gasping, as if she'd used up all the available air.

Verian gently pushed a strand of hair off her mother's face.

'You will exhaust yourself, Mama. Please stay quiet and I'll make your drink.'

Verian lifted the kettle and poured steaming water into a clay mug. The liquid fizzed as a glorious, pungent smell of herbs filled the cave. Gwen's nostrils widened at its richness.

The mother smiled at Gwen and Mark. 'I am Alethia, Truthteller, mother of Verian, also Truthteller.' Her breath caught. 'We are daughters of Truthtellers from times distant and faded in the minds of our people. Only the Truthtellers remember.'

She patted the moth-eaten furs around her. 'Sit here, and I will tell you the story of our people. But first' – she sharply drew in air – 'I am curious to know what brings you into the Deep Forest. Will you tell me?'

Verian handed over the hot drink and she, Gwen and Mark rested on the furs as Alethia took small sips.

'It's as we told the queen,' Gwen said. 'We are Danae from the Forest. Madach have come from over the sea and threaten to drive us out, like they did once before.'

'From over the sea?' Verian said. 'There are also Madach here, further into the Deep Forest. Our hunters have glimpsed them from time to time, huge and fearsome – creatures to frighten the children with.'

'And our queen,' Alethia said.

Gwen wanted to ask about the frightening Madach in the Deep Forest, but Mark said, 'There's an old, old story about the Sleih helping us once before, when the Madach forced us into the Deep Forest. So we wanted to find the Sleih, ask for help again.'

Verian and Alethia nodded as if they knew the story too.

Alethia took another sip of the herbal liquid, and in the pause Gwen heard the swish of the heavy curtain being pulled aside.

Maikin peeked into the cave.

'Ah! I wondered if you'd be here. Too bad, too bad.' He

gazed at Verian and her mother and then at Gwen and Mark. 'You must not listen to these women and their mad stories. They're all mad, all mad, from a long line of mad women.'

'We haven't been here more than a minute or two,' Gwen said curtly. She didn't at all like the way Maikin talked about Verian and Alethia. 'They've had no chance to tell us anything.'

Maikin took no offence. 'Good, good,' he said. 'And now you and your brother must come along with me, back to where I left you.' He pulled the curtain further aside. 'You shouldn't stray, not at all. It's too easy to be lost in these tunnels. What would our queen say if you were lost?'

Gwen started to protest when Verian laid a hand on her arm and gave a small shake of her head. 'Later,' she whispered.

Maikin led Gwen and Mark, like naughty children, back to the cave. 'You shouldn't wander off. You could easily become lost,' he said. 'The queen is usually quick about her decisions. You should rest, and no doubt the summons will come tomorrow, or the day after.'

He had his hand on the curtain to leave when he said, 'And you must not talk to those mad women. They are full of lies to upset our queen.' He disappeared into the passage.

'What's happening?' Mark said. 'Why are they worried about what Verian and her mother might tell us? Why pretend they're mad? They're about as mad as you and me.'

'I wish we'd been able to stay long enough to find out,' Gwen said. 'And I agree. The Truthtellers are a lot more, well, sane, than the queen.'

'What we did find out isn't good though, is it?'

'You mean about the Madach in the Deep Forest?'

'Lucy ... you don't think ...?'

Gwen's eyebrows went up. 'No! Do you think ...? No, too awful. She couldn't have been taken by Madach.'

Gwen felt sick.

Chapter Five

The Queen Decides

Breakfast – red, blue and purple wild berries and a thick, milky liquid – was brought to them by the shy boy, who again scuttled off without a word. Afterwards, Mark paced the cave, pulling aside the curtain every few minutes to peek out into the passageway. The people walking past ignored him.

Gwen, as bored as Mark, tapped her fingers on the wooden table top. She tried not to think about the weight of rock and soil hanging above her.

'How long do you think we'll have to wait?' Mark peeked between the curtains one more time.

'How would I know?'

'What if it's days? I'll go silly, cramped up in here.'

'Me too. More than silly.' Gwen glanced up to the roof. She blew out a shuddery breath.

Mark plumped onto a chair. 'We'll have to ask Maikin to lead us out of here, if the queen doesn't help us.'

'Why shouldn't she help us?'

Mark squinted at Gwen. 'It feels all wrong. The queen ...' he shrugged. 'And what Verian said about finding the Sleih, why say that if we've already found them? And what did Alethia want to tell us?' He stared at Gwen. 'There's no help here.'

There was a moment's silence. Gwen jumped from her chair and strode to the cavern opening.

'Let's find Verian and find out what's going on. If Maikin

comes looking for us, well, too bad.'

As Gwen reached for the heavy curtain Maikin emerged through the folds. Gwen jumped back into the cavern.

'Startle you?' Maikin said.

Gwen laughed shakily. 'I was about to look out for you.'

'I thought I heard my name. That'd explain it, wouldn't it?' Maikin didn't soften his words with any hint of a smile.

Gwen was saved from more lies by Mark rushing forward. 'Has the queen made a decision?'

'Yes, come along.' Maikin didn't share Mark's excitement. 'The queen has indeed made her decision.'

**

The heavy doors stood wide today, guarded by men with metal-tipped spears.

Inside, there was barely enough light to see the people standing in twos and threes around the damp walls of bare rock. Gwen lifted her eyes to the shadowy roof. Nausea roiled in her stomach. She forced her gaze down and found Verian, standing not far from the queen's throne. The girl's head was bent, her long black hair hiding her face.

The queen hunched forward on her stone chair. Her pupil-black eyes shifted from Gwen to Mark and back again. Maikin whispered in the queen's ear. She glanced sharply at Verian then back to her guests.

'You have been listening to the lurid tales of the girl, Verian, and her mad mother?' The queen's eyes were flints.

Had they already made an enemy of this queen? Gwen didn't want that.

'Majesty, we came by accident across Verian's home and she kindly invited us in. We'd been there no time at all before Maikin took us out.'

Gwen paused, as if considering. 'We would like to learn the stories of the Sleih, and especially Your Majesty's own part in those stories, which we imagine to be one of great wisdom.'

'Is that so?' the queen said, with a tiny curl of her lips. 'Good, good. There will be ample time for stories, later.' She closed her eyes, leaned into the back of her throne and drummed her fingers on its cold arms.

They waited.

'We have made our decision.' The queen's eyes flew open. She shifted forward on her throne.

When the queen didn't continue, Gwen said, 'You will help our people ... Majesty?'

'Help your people? Yes, yes, we will help your people.'

'Thank you, Majesty.' Gwen sneaked a satisfied smirk at Mark.

When the queen was not forthcoming about how she might help, Mark said, 'How, Majesty? How will you help our people?'

'Ah! Here we have the clever part.' The queen favoured them with a rigid grin, showing a row of shiny white teeth. 'We will not fight these Madach who are threatening your Danae. We would need to show ourselves, go Above Ground, into the Great Open. Too dangerous, too dangerous indeed.'

Gwen's warm satisfaction cooled.

The queen shook her head. The metal crown tipped onto her forehead and had to be thrust back into place. 'We have a much better plan.' The rigid grin grew wider. 'We are the Sleih, protectors of the Danae, and therefore we will protect you.'

The queen bent further forward. 'I will send a trusted Sleih, like Maikin here, to your people, and,' she paused, raised her voice triumphantly, 'he will bring them here!'

'Bring them here?' Mark and Gwen said together.

'Yes, yes, don't you see? If we bring them here, we can protect them, forever.'

'What the silliest ...' Mark's protest was cut off by Gwen's shove to his ribs. 'Ouch.'

'Majesty,' Gwen said, 'may we have time to think on your generous offer?'

Gwen shared Mark's amazed disbelief. She didn't want the queen angry with them, however. Whatever the queen thought about Verian's sanity, Gwen had doubts about Her Majesty.

The queen's face soured like week-old cream. 'I see no reason to think about it. Surely it's obvious. And'–she narrowed her eyes at Gwen–'while Maikin is away, you and your brother will stay here, in safety, being protected as Danae should be protected.'

She leaned towards Maikin. 'And unable to do any spying,' she whispered loudly.

'Spying? We're not spies,' Mark blurted.

'Spies everywhere,' spat the queen, 'working for those who would invade our caverns, those who plot for my throne.'

Gwen remembered Alethia saying the queen feared the Madach in the Deep Forest. They must be the plotters.

The queen lost interest in spies. Now she glared at Verian who, green eyes staring, arms outstretched, was making her way steadily to Gwen.

'Seek the Sleih, the true Sleih. Some will not care, but care they will. Some will care, but care not for you.' Verian gently touched Gwen's cheek, then dropped her hand to her side, gazing around as if awakening from a dream.

The people in the cavern murmured, shifting uneasily.

Chapter Six

The True Sleih

'The true Sleih, yes, they must seek the true Sleih.'

The queen swivelled her head towards the high, breathless voice cutting through the whispering in the cave.

'Mama!' Verian cried.

Alethia approached, barely upright, supported by two young women whose eyes were fixed on the earth floor.

'Why have you brought *her* here?' the queen shouted at the women, who jumped away from Alethia like she'd turned into a scorpion. She would have fallen except Gwen and Verian rushed to catch her.

'I persuaded them,' Alethia said. 'I told them the future of our people depended on my immediate presence in this chamber.'

'My dear Alethia,' the queen said, 'we thought you far too ill to leave your furs and leathers.' She paused. 'You should go back to them, immediately.' Her voice rose. 'One mad woman we can manage. Two is MOST TIRESOME.'

Her shout echoed in the anxious quiet of the cavern.

'Come, Mama,' Verian said. 'You should be abed, not here.'

'Young Danae,' Alethia said, 'whatever our Majesty might say, you should know we are not the Sleih.' Her deep green eyes were locked on the queen, who stared back through her own black slits. 'We are Danae, as you are.'

Gasps rose from the people standing by the damp walls.

Gwen blinked.

Not Sleih? They were Danae?

Of course – Maikin, Verian, the way they looked like her and Mark and the villagers. Mark was right about something being wrong.

The revelation brought an odd sense of relief. She and Mark would have to keep searching. But the real Sleih might help them, not like this queen.

The queen's plump fingers were white where she gripped the arms of her throne.

Mutterings arose. 'Mad, like Her Majesty says, mad.'

Alethia slowly raised one hand and the people fell silent.

'Have you all forgotten?' she said. 'Have you forgotten we have not always dwelled in the caverns?' She gulped in air. 'Once, we lived Above Ground in a beautiful land ... we grew crops and bred cattle .... and sheep and lived well.' Her head fell forward as she fought for breath.

Verian took up the story. 'Have you all forgotten? Have you forgotten how the Madach deeply desired our lands, and we, the Danae, would not be cowed? And how, in the last days, they forced us from our homes, driving us into the Deep Forest. Have you forgotten how our people journeyed for many days and many months, not all surviving, until we came here to the caverns?'

Gwen saw Mark drinking this in, a small, knowing grin on his face.

The cavern dwellers stood rigidly. Many slowly shook their heads, sighing loudly, appearing saddened by this mad tale. Others stared at Verian. Gwen noticed none dared look at the queen, who had not moved during this telling.

Alethia stopped coughing and raised her head once more.

'Young Danae,' she said to Gwen, still at her side, and Mark a few steps away, 'you must seek the true Sleih, as Verian Truthteller says. It is there you will find the help the Danae

31

need, as once before the Sleih helped our people.'

'No!' the queen barked.

She hauled herself from her throne and marched down the cavern. 'By the Beings! True Sleih, indeed! Take the *Truthtellers* out of here! I no longer want this mad woman and her mad daughter in my presence. I care not who they are.'

The cavern was a din of babbling voices. Guards rushed from the door. They wrenched Alethia and Verian away from Gwen and hustled them out of the cavern.

Gwen watched them go. She felt abandoned, lost, and exposed.

The queen stamped back to her throne.

'I told you something was wrong,' Mark murmured. 'I told you she wouldn't help us. Bring us here? Can you imagine what Tomas would have to say about bringing us here?'

'Well?' the queen said to Gwen, as if there'd been no interruption at all. 'Do you accept our offer? Or are you spies after all?'

Gwen's head and heart were with the Truthtellers. She wanted to shout at this stupid queen, tell her she was the mad one, not Alethia or Verian. Tell her that her plan for protecting the Danae was an idiot's plan and she and Mark must leave the gloomy caverns immediately and get on with their quest.

Spies. Gwen thought about it. Would this insane queen let them go? Goosebumps prickled her back.

Gwen met the queen's stare.

'Majesty,' she said, 'my brother and I thank you for your offer. Be assured we are not spies, for anyone. We are simply on a quest to seek help for our people.'

The queen's black gaze showed no sympathy.

'I fear, Majesty, your plan would not be successful.' Gwen tried to appear rueful. 'Our people will not want to leave their homes and journey here, to live in caverns under the earth. They have not been raised to the dark, as your people have.

How would they farm and work their gardens and tend their livestock?'

The queen's eyes flashed. 'It is what I offer. Take it or do not take it, I care not.' She turned to Maikin. 'Take them away, they are ungrateful Danae. Make sure they do not leave the caverns. I am convinced they are spies.'

Not leave the caverns? Gwen's back prickled with cold sweat. She wanted to cry out, No. She wanted to demand to be led up and out, into the shifting but sky-filled forest.

She calmed herself. If she resisted, made a fuss, this queen was likely to have them locked away, with no chance at all of escape.

Loud whispering followed Gwen and Mark out of the queen's chamber. Maikin herded them through the passages, none of them speaking until they reached the cave, when Mark said, 'Did you know you're not Sleih?'

Maikin growled, a sound like a dog's warning. 'Never say such a thing, never.'

Gwen's mind swirled with a longing for escape so strong it made her feel ill. But how?

'Don't wander off,' Maikin said, holding the curtain to usher them through. 'Easy to get lost.'

The cold prickles scuttling down Gwen's back grew colder.

Maikin let the curtain fall. Gwen listened to his footsteps moving heavily down the tunnel. She shivered.

'I was right, wasn't I?' Mark said. 'No help there.'

He kicked angrily at the furs on the leather mattresses, spilling them onto the earth floor.

'Are we going to spend the rest of our lives in these caves?' Mark slapped a hand against the cold rock wall.

Chill fingers tightened around Gwen's chest.

She couldn't breathe. She ran to the cavern entrance.

'We have to get out.'

Her hand tugged at the heavy curtain.

'I can't stay here, not in these caves. We have to get out. I don't care what the queen says, we have to get out.'

Chapter Seven

The Way Of The Truthtellers

'Calm down. You're worrying me,' Mark said.

Gwen didn't calm down. She darted about, gathering up their few belongings, rolling them into the tattered, dirty blankets they'd brought from home. She threw Mark his blanket roll and his cloak. 'Put them on. We're leaving.'

'Good idea,' he said, catching both. 'But how? How can we find the way out?'

'I don't know. Somehow. There must be a way, somewhere.'

'What if we get lost?'

Gwen's face paled. 'Don't say it, don't think it. Lost, underground, forever.' She pressed her hand to the wall, gasping as if winded.

'Verian,' Mark said. 'I think I can find my way to Verian's cave. She'll help us.' He checked the passage. 'Doesn't seem they're keeping any sort of guard on us.'

Gwen roughly thrust her way past Mark and into the tunnel. Mark frowned, and followed, just in time to see Gwen race around the first corner.

It was the wrong passage and he was about to call out when she came running back, panting. 'People, there are people down there. I don't think they saw me. Where do we go now?' She strained to see past Mark's shoulder, pivoted, shaking her head. 'I have to get out of here!'

'It's all right, Gwen, it's all right,' Mark said. 'It's the next tunnel, I'm sure.' He led her along, both of them running, and around the corner.

Voices sounded. Mark squashed himself against the rock wall, pulling Gwen with him. 'Sshh.'

The voices passed.

Mark took off after Gwen who was already dashing down this new tunnel, wildly glancing into every cave where the curtain was pulled aside, muttering, 'Where, where? Which one is it?'

Mark reached her, grabbed her arm. 'Stop, Gwen. Calm down. Let's do this properly. There's no need for panic.'

'No need for panic? Don't you see?' Gwen brushed at tears. 'If we don't escape, they'll lock us up. We'll be here, in these caves, for the rest of our lives.' Sweat shone on her white face.

'All will be well, Gwen. Come, we can help you. We know a way.'

'Verian.' Mark let out a breath. 'Thank the Beings. We were trying to ...'

'Verian, Verian, help us!'

Verian started when Gwen threw her arms around her, sobbing.

'I was coming to find you, to help. We must be quick.' Verian gently disentangled herself and hurried down the tunnel. 'Most are in the throne room, listening to the queen tell them how you must not be allowed outside the caverns, and how Maikin is going to find the Danae and bring them to us to protect.' She laughed softly. 'Fortunate Danae.'

They moved swiftly, turned right, right again, and fell through the curtain into Verian's cave.

Alethia rested on the scruffy leather pillows, sipping a mug of the aromatic liquid.

'Ah, Verian has found you,' she said.

Gwen sank onto the furs, gasping for breath as if she'd had to outrun bears and wolves and giant boar.

'Are you all right?' Mark said.

'Yes, yes, it was just, you know, always being down here, never seeing the sky, or a tree, or feel the rain ...' Gwen's voice quavered. 'You'll lead us out?' she said to Verian.

'Yes, yes.' Verian smiled.

'We have a way, known to none except the Truthtellers, and the queen,' Alethia said. 'You must go immediately, before Maikin discovers you are missing.'

As Alethia spoke, Mark heard voices in the passage outside. Not the normal sober voices of these underground people. Raised, excited voices.

Verian grabbed a bundle lying on the floor, pulled Gwen from the furs, and jostled her and Mark across the cave to the rocky wall. She pressed her fingers into a slim gap. Mark blinked as part of the wall disappeared, leaving a narrow, midnight-black opening.

Verian gestured for them to go through. 'Hurry.'

Mark slipped inside. Gwen stepped back, away from the opening, and Verian bundled her into the gap. Inside, Verian pushed one of the stones. The opening slowly closed.

As the last of the light from the cave shrank to nothing, Mark heard Maikin say, 'Where is Verian, Alethia? Does she have the Danae with her?'

Alethia's reply was lost in the blackness.

***

The darkness was complete. Gwen's stomach tightened as she forced down her panic.

A scratching noise, a light flared. Verian held a lamp up high. 'We must hurry,' she said, moving along the stony path with Mark behind her, Gwen following. 'The queen knows of this way and while she cannot send guards through here, she will surely send them above, to prevent our exit.'

'Alethia? Will she be all right?' Gwen's eyes never left Verian's light.

'Oh yes,' Verian said. 'She is, after all, the queen's sister, or rather half-sister. The old king was their father.'

Gwen couldn't think about this. Her chest heaved and her legs were too heavy to carry her forward.

Verian glanced over her shoulder. 'Hurry!' she said. 'We must reach there before the guards.'

Her urgency prodded rudely at Gwen's panic. Her heart thumped loudly enough she was sure Mark and Verian must hear. She stumbled on a stone, felt the rough walls closing in on either side, the roof falling, so low she must bend her head ... she had to crawl, or be trapped, lost in the dark, always ...

'Gwen.' Mark twisted in the shadows to face Gwen. 'It's fine. We're going up, to the surface. And the roof's higher, see?'

Gwen made herself stand up straight, gulped hard. 'Thank you.' Be brave, she told herself. They were getting out of this darkness.

In the gloom, constantly watching her feet, Gwen lost all sense of time. It may have been minutes or hours they scurried along like beetles in the dirt, racing to beat the guards.

At last, Verian stopped. 'We must put out the light.'

Gwen dreaded the blackness to come. Verian extinguished the lantern, the tunnel blackened. Gwen fought her dread. And realised she could see, albeit faintly. Not far ahead, light filtered through to them.

As did a dank, musty, and unfamiliar, smell.

Chapter Eight

Light And Air

'Wait here,' Verian said, running to the filtered light. She disappeared around a corner.

Mark would have run after her. Gwen held him back.

'Verian said to wait. Do you want to run straight into Maikin and be taken back down?' She shuddered. 'Because I don't.'

Mark had no time to argue. Verian re-appeared, beckoning. 'Come. Quickly.'

Gwen didn't need to be asked twice. She beat Mark to the corner where Verian waited.

'Take this, it's for the journey.' Verian thrust the small bundle she'd been carrying into Gwen's bag. 'This way,' she said.

Gwen followed Verian into a cavern where the dank, musty smell reached out to claw at her throat. Mark, coming up beside her, coughed.

The smell was forgotten at what Gwen saw through the opening across the cavern.

Trees, shadowy with coming night. Her heart lifted. She raced across the packed earth, stumbling over hard objects which rattled under her feet. She flew to the trees, and air, and out of the cave.

Verian, already outside, grabbed her arm. 'Don't move,' she said. She leaned across Gwen to do the same to Mark as he emerged into the warm evening. All three stood wedged into a crack in a wall of rock. Gwen, light-headed with relief, watched Verian scan the rock to either side of them.

'The guards have not yet come,' Verian said. 'You will have time to escape.'

She pointed at the trees which rose tall and thick a short distance off. 'Go to the oak, see there, right ahead. Take the path by its side. It will make your way easier for a time. When the moon rises, go left, into the forest, leaving the path. That way is west. Go as far as you can before you rest.'

Mark set off, hunched down, scrambling around bushes and bracken. Gwen would have followed, but Verian said, 'One thing.'

Gwen paused.

'Silver,' Verian said.

'Silver?'

'I see you with silver, in my dreams.' Verian's pale brow creased. 'I cannot see if it is for ill or for good, only that you should be wary.'

Gwen couldn't see herself having much to do with silver, or any other precious metals. There was no time to ask more. Shouts rose and flames flared from the bushes hugging the rock wall.

'The queen's guards! Go!'

Gwen crouched, running awkwardly, her eyes on where Mark already squatted by the oak. She willed him not to be seen, willed herself not to be seen. The shouting of the guards sounded loud in the twilight stillness.

Behind Gwen, too close, a different noise arose – a long, wild howl, and another. The shouts of the guards twisted to screams. Gwen's skin crawled. She reached the oak and dared to look back.

Verian stood where they'd left her, the rock behind her reddening in the sinking sun. Her hands were buried deep in the black fur of a wolf leaning into her side.

As Gwen watched, open-mouthed, the wolf lifted its long,

dark muzzle and howled. More howls answered from within the bushes. The screams from the guards rose and the flames raced through the trees, away from Verian, away from Gwen and Mark.

Verian raised a slim arm in farewell, and the wolf lifted its head, sniffing the air as if to catch a scent ... of something or someone.

Callie came to Gwen's mind. Callie, with the same sea-green eyes as Verian and her love of the forest creatures.

Mark tugged at Gwen's elbow. 'Let's go.'

Gwen raised her own arm to Verian before running after Mark, back into the Deep Forest.

***

Verian pressed her back against the warm rock. The wolf had left her, loping silently towards the flames and the screams to join the pack chasing the guards back to the caverns.

She herself must return, down through the long tunnels to her own cave, with its thin mattresses and patchy furs. She had left Alethia for too long.

One moment more.

A moment more to breath the scents of the forest, feel the breeze on her cheeks. She gazed up to the darkening sky, searching out the first of the stars.

Her mind went back to when she was a small child, when the queen was not obsessed with spies and enemies wanting to take her throne from her. To a time when Above Ground was simply another place, where the cavern dwellers farmed crops, grew vegetables, and raised livestock. Some had built homes there, coming underground when they wished to visit or to attend the queen's assemblies.

Back to the time when the underground passageways were full of light, torches all the way, the walls hung with evergreen branches from the forest, complete – Verian smiled – with squirrels and, sometimes, birds.

She remembered the earth floors covered in fresh grasses and sweet herbs where tiny forest creatures played and the people had to tread carefully. And the pots, huge to a small girl, filled with young trees, fruiting bushes, herbs and wildflowers – wild mint, tiny jewels of wild raspberries, purple bluebells, snowdrops, pink and white foxgloves. Moving through the caverns had been like walking along a woodland path.

And the poor queen. Verian sighed. Her beautiful, laughing aunt who loved to dance and to sing. And the picnics they had Above Ground, by waterfalls and streams, bathing in the hot summers alongside tumbling otters and dancing water rats.

And winter, which was almost as good as summer. For when the snows were deep, they would keep to the caverns, warm and snug, the smell of fresh cut pine filling the air.

Verian closed her eyes. 'Ah, Grandmamma, what did you do to us, when you told the queen your Truth, the Truth which drove us all into hiding?'

A wet nose nuzzled her hand. Verian reached out to pat the wolf's coarse black fur.

'Well done, thank you.'

Slowly, she made her way into the cavern, stepping between the picked-over bones scattered across the dry, hard floor, and down into the earth, to home.

***

Gwen and Mark fled, watching and listening for guards with lights and fire. The growing darkness made it difficult to go swiftly. Mark tripped over a tree root and fell heavily onto his hands. He scrambled up, grumbling about trees and the Madach could have them all if they wanted them.

'Hush,' Gwen cautioned.

The root lifted a little, and fell back to the earth when Gwen skirted around it. She found a stick to help her feel her cautious way, listening for guards, expecting to see lights and fire ahead.

Nothing. It appeared the wolves had done their job well.

The moon rose and the brightness was almost like daylight.

Gwen remembered Verian's advice. She found a grass-flattened track which must be used by animals and followed it to the left, heading west. The faint trail held but still they moved slowly between the misshapen trees, wary of shifting roots. The moon cast deep shadows where night animals scuttled out of their way. A hunting owl hooted.

When at last the moon hovered above the horizon, Gwen sank to the ground. 'I can't go any further. We must have come far enough to escape any guards.'

Mark dropped down beside her. 'Did you see the wolves? With Verian?'

'I did.' Gwen screwed up her nose at the memory of the smell and the hard bone-like objects under her feet. 'We must have run straight past them.'

'They must be Verian's friends, helping us.'

'Friends with wolves?' Gwen was uncertain about this. 'How? Wolves are wild creatures. They eat people, not make friends with them.'

'They weren't trying to eat Verian, or us.'

'Mmm. Could you ever trust them?'

'Hope I don't have to find out,' Mark said, rummaging about in Gwen's bag. 'What was it Verian gave you? Is it anything we can eat?' He lifted out the leather bundle, untied it and held up a small stone bottle.

'What's this?' He pulled the stopper and a sharp aroma of herbs billowed into the night air.

Gwen inhaled deeply. 'Smells like the medicine Verian gives her mother.'

Mark took a small sip of the liquid. 'Mmm. It's good.'

'Special too, I suspect. Best we keep it for later, because, see, there's food here too.' Gwen pulled out two small cakes from a batch nestled in a cloth bag.

The fresh flavour of the cakes more than made up for their

hard, rough texture. Gwen and Mark ate them sitting beneath the long branches of a willow.

Gwen's eyelids drooped. 'We should sleep.'

Mark was already curled in his cloak, head on his shoulder, softly snoring.

Gwen wrapped her cloak about her, wriggling to find a comfortable position on the grassy earth. She thought of the feather-filled leather mattress, and sighed at the relief of being out of the caverns, feather mattresses or not.

Chapter Nine

The Blue Lady

The rabble of children running around the fire came to a sudden halt. The dogs lay on their bellies in the dirt, ears back. The men, women and older children stood frozen in whatever they were doing. A woman carrying two pails of water grimaced at their weight, but made no effort to put the pails down.

Isa, as motionless as the others, watched the lady ride into the camp. The lady's horse was tall, black and handsome, with brightly painted hooves which danced on the dusty ground as if about to take flight. The lady herself was the most beautiful person Isa had ever seen, slimly built, skin the colour of pale honey and shining black hair neatly braided high on her head. Blue and white precious stones which out-glittered the summer sun were tucked into the braids. The lady held herself erect in her ornately worked saddle. The soft rich cloth of her blue dress fell smoothly over her knees to the silver-tipped toes of her dainty boots.

Part of Isa didn't understand why the lady hadn't been taken from her horse and her jewels removed from her hair. Part of her suspected anyone fool enough to try might find themselves in trouble, although the lady carried no weapon which Isa could see, bar a short riding crop.

The beautiful lady eyed the people of the camp as they eyed her. Except, Isa realised, their mouths were open in awe, while the lady's red lips were pinched together in contempt.

Isa's own mouth fell open when the lady's sea-green eyes flashed at her.

'Who's in charge, girl?' The lady tapped the crop lightly across the black horse's neck. The horse lifted its sculptured head. The dogs sank further into the dirt. 'I need to speak to whoever is in charge of this Madach rabble. Now.'

Isa's mind was a cloud of confusion. She opened her mouth wider. No sound came out.

'We have no one in charge of us,' a gruff voice said.

Isa recognised the voice as Chester's, a solid man of middle age respected for his strength, both of body and mind. He stood by the open flap of his tent, one hand pushing back his long, greying blonde hair. He was the one person in the camp not over-awed by the presence of the Blue Lady, as Isa would forever think of her.

The lady dropped from her horse, left its reins to trail on the ground and strode swiftly to Chester.

'Your Madach travel this forest, do they not?'

The lady was much shorter than Chester. She had to tilt her head back to stare up at him. It didn't make the lady seem any weaker.

Chester nodded.

'I need you to find something for me.'

Chester kept nodding.

'Danae.'

Isa's eyes grew round. Danae? They were an old fairytale. What did the lady mean?

'Danae?' Chester said. 'What about 'em?'

'I believe there are two Danae children travelling these forests. I must have them.'

'The Danae are a fairytale.' Chester crossed his arms and stared at the lady. Her sea-green eyes bore into his brown ones. He didn't flinch although a faint sheen of sweat glistened on his forehead.

The lady's riding crop whistled close to Chester's leg. 'Fairytale or not,' she said, 'I want them. They are of great value to me.'

At a sign from the lady, her horse stepped to her side. She gracefully lifted herself into the saddle. The horse's hooves pranced in the dirt, the dogs squirmed, and the lady patted the plaited mane.

'If you find them, or hear word of them, send a message to the Citadel of Ilatias, to Lady Melda of the House of Alder.' She turned the black horse towards the trees. 'I will come.'

The lady cantered out of the camp in a spray of dust. The dogs rose up, hackles stiff, growling, staring into the forest. None of them made any move to chase after the black horse and its rider.

Isa watched the lady melt into the forest. She wriggled her stiff shoulders and glanced at Chester. His arms remained folded, his heavy grey brows drawn together.

'Who was she?' The woman with the pails of water at last lowered them to the ground and rubbed her aching arms.

Chester took a long time to answer. When he spoke his voice was hesitant. 'A Sleih lady, from the Citadel, it seems.'

Someone said, 'The Citadel's many days' journey from here.'

Chester blinked, as if coming out of a trance. 'She must be properly anxious to have these Danae children if she's cast her net so wide.' He grinned. 'Well, if we find 'em, if they exist, we'll make her pay a good price for 'em.'

'Could've got a good price for all those jewels in her hair, and for her horse as well,' a stocky young man said. His friends about him murmured their agreement.

Chester faced the murmurers. 'Didn't see any of you brave young warriors trying to relieve her of her jewels.'

There were grumblings, something about whips. Chester gave a scornful snigger and went back to his tent.

Isa gazed towards the forest, thinking about the lady and her strange request. She hoped Da and Uncle Viv would come back from their hunting trip soon. She couldn't wait to tell Da about the Blue Lady's visit.

Chapter Ten

Dreams?

A fluttering like the wings of a languid butterfly stroked Gwen's sleeping cheek. She stirred in her cloak and lifted an unconscious hand to her face.

The fluttering wings tinkled in her ear, a tiny bell. Gwen blinked open one eye. She was dreaming. She thought she'd grown used to the night noises of this unfriendly forest – the soughing which may or may not be the wind in the treetops, the trembling whistling which may or may not be night birds, or the smothered scratchings of prey burrowing under rotting roots.

This tinkling was a different sound, a man-made sound.

Gwen opened both eyes, closed them briefly and opened them again. She freed her arms from her tangled cloak and sat up.

'Oh!'

The round eyes of an elfin face, half hidden by a mass of curls gleaming silver in the starlight, stared at Gwen.

'Who are you?'

The girl laughed and the tinkling sounded again.

'What's happening? Gwen? Who are you talking ...? Oh.' Mark heaved himself upright.

'It's a girl,' he said.

Gwen nodded. 'A Danae girl.'

The girl was very young, younger than Callie. Her knee-length dress, pale in the starlight, swirled gently about her legs in a breeze Gwen couldn't feel. She gazed dreamily from Gwen to Mark with eyes which were a little too large for her fine-featured face, and deeply dark.

'Who are you? Where have you come from?' Gwen said. 'Where's your ma and da? Where's your family?'

'Here,' the girl whispered. She lifted an arm to indicate the forest all around them.

'Are you Danae?' Mark said.

'Danae? Danae!' There was the tinkling laughter. 'Yes, yes, Danae.'

'And your family's nearby?'

'Yes, yes. Come, come with me. See them, see my family.'

Gwen frowned at Mark. 'Is this going to end up with me in a pitch black hole underground?'

Mark was already standing. 'No caves here, and if there are, well, we can just refuse to go.' He hefted his bag onto his shoulder. 'On the other hand, we might find someone who knows about the Sleih and can help us find them. Don't know about you, but I'm tired of wandering around this strange forest with no idea where we're going.'

Gwen stood too, wary eyes on the elfin girl. 'I don't know. She doesn't look, well, quite right, to me.'

'It's this dull light. It'll be day soon and we'll be able to see her properly. Come on, let's go,' Mark urged, for the girl was skipping with slow, unhurried skips into the trees.

Gwen picked up her bags and followed.

***

When would it be day?

Gwen was certain it must be well past the time when dawn should have broken. But the light hadn't changed. There was no birdsong.

The silence was as deep as midnight. Not as dark, though. Starlight gleamed on their guide's bobbing curls and the way ahead was marked, faintly, by a faded path which wended its narrow way, back and forth, around stands of ferns and wide-girthed oaks and tall beeches whose higher branches were lost in a murky gloom.

They were lost.

They were already lost, so what did it matter?

The girl halted at a stream flowing silently across their way. A low grassy bank led down to the dark waters.

'Are we nearly there?' Mark said. 'Is your family close by?'

'There.' The girl pointed across the stream.

Gwen shivered. Despite the warm summer night, her skin was cold, prickled with goosebumps as if a damp mist had wrapped itself around her.

'Are we meant to cross over? Is it deep?' Mark kept asking questions.

'Not deep, no, see.' The girl walked into the stream. Her boots slid into its inky waters with no break in the smoothly running surface.

Gwen wondered how deep the stream was. The girl walked confidently into the middle of the current, paused to glance over her shoulder, and was soon on the far shore.

The water hadn't reached to her knees.

Mark had stepped down the bank, poised to follow.

'Take your boots off,' Gwen said, sitting to remove her own boots.

Mark pulled off his boots, tied the laces and threw them across his shoulder. Gwen did the same, aware of the girl watching from the far bank of the dark stream.

'Here we go,' Mark said. 'Doesn't look any worse than the hundreds of other streams we've crossed.'

Gwen didn't share his certainty. Streams which could be easily waded were, in her experience, dancing waters curving noisily around rocks, pulling at her bare toes, silken mosses taunting her with their slipperiness. Not smoothly silent like this stream.

Mark waded in. 'Ow! It's freezing.'

He took long strides, trying to hurry, pushing hard against the stream's flow. It didn't work. Rather, he appeared to find every step difficult, like straining through a snow drift. His breath rasped loudly in the hushed forest.

How had the girl crossed so easily?

The girl watched. Her pale dress lifted in the unfelt breeze, her silvered hair gleamed like a lantern.

Gwen took a breath and placed one foot in the stream. She gasped at the iciness, found herself wading slowly through water heavy as honey. She kept her eyes fixed on Mark, who had reached the far shore.

He gazed back at her, unsmiling, making no jokes about the coldness or the force of the noiseless stream.

Gwen stared at him. His boots dangled over his shoulder.

Why was he silent? Why hadn't he put his boots on?

The eerie quiet and the pale darkness were oppressive. Gwen felt as if someone had thrown a heavy blanket over her. Her heart slowed. Her skin grew as cold as her bare toes. Her arms and legs were leaden.

She reached the bank and lifted a hand to Mark, wanting help to get out of the water.

He turned his back on her.

The girl was skipping her languorous skips along the faint path between the dark trees. Mark followed her.

Gwen's heart burst back into life as she hauled herself from the stream. There was danger in those trees. More than the ever present danger of twisting roots and spiralling low branches catching at her hair and clothes.

She wanted to shout, 'No, don't follow her!'

Her mouth wouldn't form the words. Her mind lost them even as she tried to cry out.

Gwen trailed, barefoot, along the hazy path behind Mark

and the girl, fighting the dimming of her thoughts, chilled to her inner soul by the coldness from the stream and the hushed twilight of the forest.

***

Mark didn't know where he was or why he was following a small Danae girl through the trees. His head was thick with soft, curling wool. He was cold. He walked behind the girl for a long time. Or a short time. He couldn't tell and it didn't matter. He wondered once when the sun would come up. And then forgot about the sun. The shadowy, silvered forest was the only place he'd ever known.

The girl stopped. 'My family, here.'

Mark stopped too. Someone – did he know the person? – stopped beside him.

'Come closer, see them.' The girl beckoned with a thin, white finger which she pointed downwards, behind her.

Mark moved forward, together with the person next to him. His gaze followed the girl's finger and even in his dreamlike state his eyes widened.

She was pointing into the black nothingness of a pit, a yawning gap which slashed the forest floor in each direction for as far as the night would let him see. It was far too wide to jump.

The person beside him said, 'Down there? They're down there?' Her tone was breathless and she stuttered the words as if she had to force them from her mouth.

'Yes, yes, Danae there. Come, meet my family.'

The girl's too large eyes locked with Mark's. He knew he would sink into those eyes, as he would sink into the black pit.

But it was what he wanted to do.

There would be rest down there. He needed rest, from the endless trekking and the futile searching for ... for something ... whatever it was. The pit would wrap him in its dark comfort, would rock him to sleep and dreams ... He moved a step closer to the edge of the pit, leaned forward, wanting to fall ...

***

Gwen stared into the pit, aware of the girl's eyes fixed on the boy beside her. Her mind struggled to escape the wet clouds smothering her thoughts.

Something was wrong.

She closed her eyes, holding the warning morsel close.

'Aaaggh! Get off me!'

The boy cried out. Gwen knew this boy. She knew ... She swung towards the cry as long brown feathers whipped at her face. Wings encircled her, clamping her arms tight to her sides. Gwen cried out too.

Shrill calls and shrieks splintered the sullen quiet.

Gwen struggled to escape the wings, uselessly. She was forced backwards, away from the pit. Her body was lifted from the ground. The wings released her. She fell to her knees, bent over, gulping in air, her lungs bursting as if she'd been running for her life.

Mark lay on the grass a short distance away, coughing and wheezing.

***

The warm summer air instantly banished Gwen's deathly chill. The sun glowed bright and high in a brilliant sky. Birds quarrelled and fussed, filling the forest with their boisterous comfort.

'Eagles.' Elbows to his sides, Mark flapped his arms in short, rapid bursts. 'Huge eagles. They attacked us.'

'Attacked us?' Gwen sat on the scrubby grass, her breathing slowing.

'I was about to find a way across the chasm, there.' Mark pointed to the wide and crooked gap opening ahead of them, an uncrossable line disappearing to either side. 'The eagles came out of nowhere and pushed me down.'

Gwen ventured close to the chasm. On the far side, stunted bushes and colourful wildflowers clung to rocky walls which plunged steeply down. She crept as near to the edge as she dared, lay on her stomach and peered over. A long way down, a tangled mass of leaves and branches hid the bottom of the gully.

'Mark, how did we get here?'

'Get here? Well, we walked, like we always do. What do you mean, how did we get here?'

Gwen wriggled back from the gap. 'I can't remember waking up, or having breakfast, or starting out today. It's like the morning never existed.'

'Umm. Well, we woke up early … it was dark I think … and … and … I don't remember having breakfast …' Mark stared into the blackness of the chasm.

'A dream,' Gwen said. 'I remember a dream, with a little girl in it.' She paused. 'I can't remember what happened in the dream.'

'You sound like Callie, talking about dreams.'

They stood silently.

Finally, Mark said, 'I'm sure we didn't have breakfast. I'm starving.' He glanced up at the midday sun. 'Time for lunch anyway. Let's eat and wait to see which way is west. It'd be good to know if we have to cross this chasm somehow or go another way.'

'The eagles … ' The lost morning nagged at Gwen. 'We were at the edge, right at the edge, and about to fall in. Everything was dark.'

'And?'

'I don't remember anything else.' Gwen waved a shaky hand at the chasm. 'If it wasn't for the eagles, we'd be down there. Dead.'

Chapter Eleven

Crossings

West was directly across the chasm.

'Of course.' Mark kicked at a stone.

'There's got to be a way over somewhere.' Gwen packed up the remains of Verian's cakes, conscious of how little was left. It would be back to nettle soup soon.

'Let's try going north and see what happens.'

Their way north was clear, through long grass and wildflowers alive with insects. Sometimes they had to detour around scrubby trees or small boulders which threatened to tumble over the edge of the chasm to crash into the greenery below. The chasm kept a straight line, with no fortunate veering westward.

In the hot afternoon, Gwen wished they would come across a stream to refill their water bottles and cool their feet.

A stream? They crossed a stream not long ago. Didn't they?

She trudged on, glancing from time to time at the sun blazing to her left as if to say, 'You should be heading this way. What's the problem?'

The sun had given up its summons and was lowering itself to the trees when Mark, ahead of Gwen, stopped and pointed. 'Look, a bridge.'

Gwen looked. Her heart faltered. 'A bridge?'

The derelict structure could be called a bridge only because it spanned the distance, more or less. Broken lengths of railing were supported here and there by the occasional crumbling stone post rising from the rotting remains of wooden planks. Mostly, the bridge was jagged holes.

'I can see a way across,' Mark said, 'if we stick close to the edge. We might have to jump the bigger holes.'

'Will it hold our weight?' Gwen tried to stop the tremor in her voice. 'Don't you think we should go on, look for somewhere else?'

She knew in her heart there was nowhere else.

'What's over there?' Mark shaded his eyes against the lowering sun to scan the far side of the bridge. 'Looks like animals. Oh, it's a fox. No, it's a family of foxes.'

Gwen squinted into the evening brightness. 'What are they doing?'

'Coming across.'

And the foxes did. With no sign of fear, either of the dilapidated crossing or of the children, they trotted swiftly across the bridge, jumping holes, pattering along the rotting planks, staying close to the edges as Mark had suggested.

Gwen and Mark made way for the family. The cubs and one of the adults scampered past and disappeared into the forest. The second adult slowed as it went by. It flicked its tail and, Gwen was certain, grinned at her before running into the trees.

'The fox grinned at me.'

Mark ignored her. 'It means the bridge is safe, if the foxes could cross.' He laughed. 'What a piece of luck! They've shown us we can go too, don't you see?'

'Do four foxes weigh as much as the two of us?'

'One of us. One at a time would be best. I'll go first, find the best way.'

Mark placed one foot on the nearest jagged plank with more confidence than Gwen thought wise. He used a short stretch of railing to inch his way forward.

Gwen held her breath, closing her eyes each time Mark came to a gap where he had to jump. Often there was no railing and she waited, heart pounding, for his screaming fall into the abyss.

He was over, waving to her. 'Come on, it's easy, honestly, as long as you watch where you're going.'

Watch where she was going? Did he think she planned to skip across?

Gwen hoisted her blanket roll and bags, clasped the piece of railing with one sweaty hand and stepped out. The sun was sinking below the trees and the broken railings and posts threw shadows across the bridge's rotten surface. It was hard to tell where solid wood or stone ended and holes began.

The chasm below was darkening rapidly.

Might be a good thing, not being able to see all the way down.

Gwen held on to the thought, looking straight ahead, judging the distances, placing one tentative boot after the other.

Time stopped.

Her face dripped with sweat. Her knees trembled.

She couldn't do it.

'You're doing well, Gwen. Keep going, don't stop, and don't look down.'

Gwen looked down, and froze.

What?

Her arm flailed about. Her hand found and clutched a stone post.

What was it, down there?

Gwen held tight to the post and squinted into the shadowy chasm.

She gasped.

A broken wheel, like a wagon wheel, hung on a high branch. Its spokeless rim rocked slowly, up and down, above the leafy canopy. A little girl in a pale dress perched on the wheel. Her mass of silver curls gleamed in the dusky shadows.

The girl stretched out a white hand and beckoned. 'Meet my family,' she called, in a high, thin voice which barely reached Gwen's dazed ears.

'Gwen, what are you doing? Keep moving, else you'll be stuck there in the dark.'

Mark's urgency broke through Gwen's shock. She clasped the stone with both hands, lifted her head – and looked down again.

The wagon wheel was there, caught in the branches. Nothing else.

Shadows, only shadows.

Gwen concentrated on Mark. Not far to go. She could see the way.

One step, a hop, a longer jump, holding on to a quivering rail, and she was over.

Gwen took three more steps and sank to the grass. Her legs were jelly.

'I saw her,' she said. 'The girl in my dream. It was the girl in my dream. Down there, in the chasm.' She drew a shuddering breath. 'She was sitting on a broken wagon wheel.'

'Is that what it was? I saw something in the treetops. Couldn't work it out. Yes, a wagon wheel, I can see now.'

'The girl? Did you see her too?'

'Girl? No, no girl.'

The forest night fell around them and it would soon be dark as black velvet. Mark gathered twigs and branches to light a fire. Gwen dug inside her bag for food.

They sat side by side, wrapped in their cloaks. The tiny fire crackled cheerfully.

Gwen's mind was still on the Danae girl. She remembered the tale of how the Danae came to the Forest, with its often repeated phrase about 'those who survived the journey'.

'Do you think,' she said, 'the wheel could have come from

one of the Danae wagons, when our people were trying to find their way through the Deep Forest?'

'Possible.' Mark chewed a hard biscuit. 'Sad to think people must have been on it. They must have tried to cross the bridge – it wouldn't have been as ruined I suppose – and toppled through the railing.'

'Yes, with a little girl falling with it.'

Gwen shivered despite the fire and her cloak. She made a silent vow. Such a fate would never befall the Danae a second time.

Chapter Twelve

Rivers And Robbers

Right foot down, left foot down, watch out for the tree root, don't let the nettles sting. Mark was sure his whole life had been spent struggling through prickly bushes which tore at his shirt and trousers and around trees whose snaking roots coiled themselves about his ankles before letting go with a slithery touch like cold, soapy fingers. He'd climbed rocky hills where the stones rolled away under his worn boots, forcing him to his hands and knees to reach the crest, and slid down grassy slopes where sharp stones attacked his backside.

At least today it wasn't raining. And the trees were less troublesome. Mark thought about it – since they'd crossed the chasm they'd not had a night where they'd woken under a different tree, and the roots he'd stumbled on had been because of his own clumsiness. Did it mean anything? He didn't care, as long as it stayed that way.

He and Gwen picked their way uphill, scrambling through heavy brush, taking the easiest route. The afternoon sun was directly ahead. Gwen, a few paces in front, stopped on a ridge and shaded her face with her hand.

Mark saw her shoulders slump. He came up beside her. A river crossed their way westward. A river which was far too wide to swim or wade.

'That's all we need.' Gwen glared at the obstructive river. 'North or south?'

'What do you mean?'

'Do we go north or south?' Gwen said. 'We can't go across unless you can see a miraculous boat somewhere.'

'Oh, I see what you mean. Not a clue.'

'Useful, thank you.'

They watched the river flow steadily south.

'Upstream might be better, because it's probably wider and faster downstream,' Gwen said.

'There might be a ford downstream.'

'There might be a ford upstream.'

They glared at each other.

'Fine,' Gwen said. 'Let's find somewhere to camp. We'll decide in the morning.'

It was an easy climb down the slope to the river, with the trees widely spaced amid low grasses coloured with pink and yellow and purple wildflowers. The evening sun sparkled off the gentle swell of the water. Birds called, bidding their good nights. High above, an eagle spiralled languidly on the warm breezes before plunging into the forest on the far side of the river.

The abrupt dive caught Mark's eye.

Wings. He and Gwen needed wings.

They set up camp beneath a chestnut tree. Supper was a handful of wild raspberries and the last drops of Verian's herbal liquid which Mark managed to shake from the stone bottle. A fire coaxed from twigs and last autumn's leaves gave little comfort in the dark night.

***

The low growl broke Gwen's sleep. Her eyes flew open. Had she dreamed it? Beside her, Mark stirred, didn't wake.

There was no moon and no stars. The night was close and humid. Gwen shivered despite the warmth. She pulled her blanket up to her chin, pummelled her scrunched up cloak which she was using for a pillow and closed her eyes. She listened.

A long howl went up, close by. It was answered by another, more distant.

Wolves. Good or bad?

Sleep came slowly.

***

The river hadn't narrowed during the night. Gwen stood on the bank, Mark beside her, watching the swirling brown water.

'North.' Gwen didn't wait for Mark's agreement. She set off along the bank, wading through long grass and around trees and bushes. A light rain fell, heavy enough to soak their cloaks and threaten to wet them all the way through if it didn't stop soon. It did stop, finally, the sun appearing from behind a white-edged cloud to decorate the forest leaves with silver glitter.

Gwen gazed up to the sky. 'We're going east.' She stamped her foot. 'We could end up right back in the village if we follow this river.'

Mark sighed loudly. 'Good.'

'Sshh.'

'What?'

'Sshh. There's something or someone ... over there!'

Gwen screamed.

'Aha!' A tall Madach with tangled brown strings of hair jumped out in front of them. Two bright red lips grinned at Gwen from beneath a stringy moustache. Two grimy hands reached out to grab her.

Gwen ducked and ran, straight into another Madach. This one was shorter and fatter, squinty-eyed and with black hair which seemed to have been cropped by sheep. He too grinned, thin pale lips bared across yellow teeth.

'Lost, kiddies?' The stringy-haired Madach clapped his hands to his knees to peer into Gwen and Mark's white faces.

'You're a long way from home, having to camp out under the stars,' the fat Madach said.

Gwen's legs shook. The big, wicked Madach ...

'I think you should come with us.' The stringy-haired Madach lunged for Mark.

Mark struggled. He tried to bite the Madach's hand, but the Madach caught and wrung his arm. Mark yelped.

'Leave him alone, you're hurting him!'

Gwen yelped too when the fat Madach squashed her hands together in his own huge, damp ones. Gwen glared up at him, and had to turn her head from his swampy breath.

'Who are you, anyway?' The Madach bent sideways to squint into Gwen's averted face.

'And where you from?' the stringy-haired Madach said.

'We're Danae, from the Forest, by the sea ...' Mark had given up struggling. He stared like a mouse transfixed by a cat.

Gwen found her nerve. 'Our village is just over there!' She tilted her head in a random direction. 'If we're not home soon our father and big brothers will worry. They're probably out looking for us right now!' She glowered at the bad-smelling fat Madach, despite her thudding heart.

The stringy-haired Madach smirked. 'Good story, girlie, except we know there're no villages for a long way about.' He prodded at Mark with his huge foot. 'I guess this urchin is telling the truth, eh?'

Gwen kicked out, squirming to escape. The fat Madach pulled at her hands, wrenching her arms. She squealed.

'Danae?' The stringy-haired Madach had his long hands clamped to Mark's thin shoulders. 'Truly? Danae?' He hunched down, his red lips open to help him better examine Mark's ashen face. 'Thought they was fairytales.'

Fairytales? Gwen's thudding heart contracted.

Like the Madach invaders believed.

Like Callie's nightmares ... Madach with whips calling about fairytales.

And Verian.

'Well well well. Look what we got ourselves.' The stringy-haired Madach smirked at his friend. 'If these two are real Danae, they'll fetch real good prices. Fairy people.' He rolled his bulging eyes. 'Who would've known?' He poked Mark with a dirty-nailed finger. 'And there's more of you? By the sea?'

'We've nothing of value.' Gwen tried to stop her voice shaking. 'We're not worth robbing. Please let us go.'

'No, you're not worth robbing,' the stringy-haired Madach said. 'You're worth something though, probably a lot of something.'

The fat Madach jerked Gwen's arms. 'Whatever you are, let's get going.'

Keeping tight hold of Gwen, he started to walk, as fast as the bushes and long grass allowed, along the bank.

Mark gasped and Gwen twisted around to see him being hauled along by the stringy-haired Madach. He stumbled and the Madach jerked him upright.

'Leave him alone, you bullies!' Gwen cried out.

The fat Madach shoved her hard between the shoulders. 'Stop it and behave, else it'll be the worse for both of you.'

Gwen couldn't see Mark, only hear his yelps of pain. She was pushed and shoved, barely kept from falling by the Madach's strong grip.

'Here we go.'

The fat Madach pushed Gwen into a small rowing boat tied to the riverbank. His stringy-haired friend threw a red-faced Mark on top of her and stepped in after them. The boat swayed.

The fat Madach gingerly followed, settled himself on the narrow seat and began to row across the river.

The Madach had chosen to cross where the river narrowed and the already swift stream ran faster.

'Watch out!' the stringy-haired Madach shouted.

A gigantic log, leafy branches thrusting in all directions,

swirled towards the boat.

Gwen held on grimly as the log struck. The boat spun about.

There was a shriek, a splash. Gwen blinked the spray of water from her eyes.

'Help!'

'Mark!' Gwen stared at the spot where Mark had been a moment before. Fear squeezed her heart.

'Gwen, help!'

Gwen threw herself at the side of the swaying boat. She reached for Mark over the roiling river. 'Here, hang on to me!'

He stretched out his arm, just as a branch of the log forced him under the water. Gwen leaned out further, the boat tipped violently and both Madach shouted as they threatened to capsize. Gwen held her breath until she saw Mark's head rise. He was much further away, the torrent hurling him rapidly downstream.

'Save him, save him,' she screamed, at the river, at the Madach, at the boat.

She tried to stand, the boat tilted harder. The stringy-haired Madach hauled her down into the wetness at the bottom.

'You trying to get us all drowned?'

'There!' Gwen pointed to where, far down the swift stream, a copper-coloured head bobbed in the currents. 'There he is, hurry!'

The Madach were too busy with the spinning boat to look out for Mark. The stringy-haired one gripped the side, one-handedly forcing back the thrusting branches. The other strained at the oars. Gwen grabbed and pushed at branches, frantic with dread. Untangled at last, the boat flew downstream.

Gwen tried to keep Mark's copper head in sight. She lost him, kept searching, heart thudding.

The Madach at the oars hauled hard – to the shore.

'What are you doing?' Gwen lurched forward, grasped at an oar.

The Madach swore and used the oar to punch her backwards. The stringy-haired Madach caught Gwen and wrapped his arms tight around her.

Gwen's screams sent the birds in the trees fluttering skywards in terror.

Chapter Thirteen

Isa And Wolves

The fat Madach pulled the boat onto a sandy strip of shore. His friend dumped Gwen over the side, punching the air from her body. Gasping, she scrambled to her feet and ran, downstream, dodging between the trees.

The stringy-haired Madach quickly caught her. He pressed Gwen's flailing arms to her sides and carried her back to the boat.

'No point, girlie,' the fat Madach said. 'And we're as sorry as you, but I'm afraid your brother won't be coming with us after all. Nasty falls not far down there. Nasty.'

'No!'

The stringy-haired Madach pushed Gwen onto a path twisting between the trees. She kicked and squirmed.

'We have to find him!'

It was no good. The Madach's grip tightened and Gwen was hustled, crying and stumbling, into the forest.

The Madach hurried along small trails, up a steep slope and down into a valley where Gwen was dragged across a shallow stream. She tripped and staggered, barely able to keep up with her captors' long-legged strides.

Mark!

Streaming tears blinded her. Gwen didn't care where she was being taken.

***

Mark's lungs burned. A rushing wetness thundered in his ears. He pushed, with his feet, with his arms, praying to the Beings he was pushing up, to the surface, and air.

He broke free, gasped, gulped more water as the river whirled him around and around. The current drew him under. He fought the fast waters. It was too hard. He had no strength. His sodden cloak wrapped itself around him as the relentless river drove him down.

Mark jerked as something caught at his hood and pulled it tight, felt his exhausted body tugged against the river's force. His head broke the surface. He gagged, spewing out water. A roaring filled his skull. The air was wet around him, choking his desperate gasps.

The grip on his cloak loosened and something wet and warm and soft clamped itself around his arm, pulling him up, up and out, out of the water, further up, onto dry land.

Mark lay on his stomach on sun-warmed stones and closed his eyes. He gulped deep breaths of dry air. He was out of the river, alive. Below him, the torrent of the waterfall roared on.

He lifted his head to find his rescuer.

Two glowing points of red, either side of a long, black and hairy nose, stared into his face.

Mark stopped breathing.

The nose moved towards him. Black jaws opened to show two rows of sharp white teeth and a long red tongue.

Mark closed his eyes, tight. He hadn't been rescued, he'd been hunted. He was about to be a wolf's dinner.

The wolf gently licked Mark's cheek, shook out its wet hair, lay down, and fell asleep.

Mark didn't dare stir.

The fight with the river, the warm pebbles, the bright sun on the back of his wet head, all took their toll. Mark slept too.

***

The setting sun glowed red through the trees when the Madach finally hustled Gwen into a sprawling camp of dirty, patched tents. Men, women and children sat on stools outside the tents or walked about looking busy. Others squatted by a fire in the middle of the camp where a huge black pot bubbled. Gwen's stomach heaved at the rich gamy smell wafting from the pot.

The fat Madach pulled her across the camp to a small tree, calling out as he went for a rope. A girl with tangled reddish hair and freckles across her grubby face ran up, a rope across her skinny arms.

She handed the rope over, gaping at Gwen. 'Who is she, Da? Where did you find her?'

The fat Madach crouched down to tie Gwen to the tree. 'Your Uncle Viv and me found her wandering by the river, lost like, and brought her here thinking to look after her for a bit.'

He pulled at the knot. Gwen winced. 'We actually had two of them,' he said. 'But the boy fell out of the boat, going across the river.'

'He drowned?' The girl glanced at Gwen, tied to the tree, ankles and hands bound in front of her, silent tears wetting her cheeks. 'Are you gonna sell this one?'

'Sure we are, Isa, and do you know'—the fat Madach stood up and beamed at the freckle-faced girl—'I reckon we'll get real gold for her.' He winked at Gwen. 'The boy told us they're Danae, you know, like the fairytale.'

'Danae? Like the lady wants?'

'Lady? What you talking about?'

'The one who wants the Danae children. She came here, beautiful she was, while you were gone. She spoke to Chester.'

'Did she now?'

The girl squinted at Gwen. 'Shame we can't keep her. If we could've, I'd have taken care of her. Honestly I would've, Da.'

'Of course we can't keep her, she's worth money, and money is what we need, not playmates for you.' The fat Madach cuffed the girl's ears. 'Come on, then. If you're good I'll let you feed her.'

The girl gawked at Gwen, who stared back through wet eyes. At another shout from her da, the girl sighed and stomped after him to the worn tents.

***

Feed her? Like pets, or animals?

Gwen's sick feeling worsened.

Mark shouldn't have told them they were Danae. Mark ...

Gwen squeezed her eyes shut, to stop more tears. She couldn't stop her thoughts though.

Mark drowned. Herself sold, a fairytale slave. Neither of them ever to see their mother and Callie again, never to find Lucy.

Lucy! Did this happen to Lucy?

And the villagers at home ... the thought was a physical pain in Gwen's chest ... would the Madach who'd come to the Forest steal the Danae away now they'd found them? Is this what Callie's dreams, what Verian's visions, meant?

The sobs threatened. Gwen forced them back.

The girl, Isa, appeared, carrying a wooden bowl. Its smelly contents sloshed over the sides.

'Dinner for the Danae.' She giggled.

Gwen hated Isa with a viciousness which surprised her. After all, it wasn't the girl's fault Mark had, Mark had ... She gulped.

Isa put the bowl on the ground. 'Wish he'd let me keep you.' She sighed. 'He won't. You're worth too much.' She gently stroked Gwen's dirty brown hair.

Gwen jerked her head and Isa sprang back.

'Hurry up there, Isa,' a woman by the fire called.

Isa picked up the bowl and warily placed it into Gwen's bound hands before walking away, looking back over her shoulder as she went.

Gwen let the bowl fall to the ground, uncaring of the

71

dark, wet stain its contents left on her already filthy trousers. Sometime later, Isa returned, gazed wistfully at Gwen and silently took the empty bowl.

Not long after, the stringy-haired Madach wandered over and checked Gwen's ropes. He carried a rough blanket. 'You'll need this.' He threw the blanket over Gwen and ambled back to the fire.

Gwen slumped against the tree, weary, yet wide awake. Mark's copper head bobbing in the river currents played over and over in her mind, along with the thunderous rush of the swirling water. Her overwrought imagination leaped to the waterfall and Mark tumbling ... no, no.

Gwen rubbed her bound wrists together until her skin tore. The rope held. She kept rubbing. Desperate tears filled her eyes.

'Well, I say we should tell her we've got her Danae!'

Gwen's ears pricked at the shout. She stared at the fire, where the shout had come from.

A solid Madach with long, greying blonde hair waved his arms about.

'It's trouble to defy her, I can feel it.' He marched off to a tent at the far side of the camp, stooped to enter, apparently changed his mind and marched back to the fire.

'You weren't here when she came.' He jabbed his finger at Gwen's captors. 'Not you, Manny, or you, Viv. You don't understand!'

The fat Madach, Isa's Da, jabbed a finger back. 'She's mine and Viv's,' he shouted. 'And what we wanna do with her is what'll happen!'

The solid Madach threw up his hands. 'You'll see, Manny, you'll see.' He disappeared into his tent.

The camp quietened. Gwen's fitful sleep was troubled by roaring rivers, crashing waterfalls, and of a low, deep growl coming from the woods at the edge of the camp.

Chapter Fourteen

Rescue

The shadows of the trees fell long over the cove where Mark lay. The pebbles had grown cool when he woke, shivering.

'Cloak.' He sleepily reached out a hand to wrap himself more tightly.

The hand caressed coarse fur.

Mark's eyes opened. He froze.

Something warm brushed against his leg.

'Ahh!'

Mark jumped up. His wet boots scrabbled on the loose stones and he fell to his hands and knees.

The wolf, startled, sprang up too, growling. Its eyes glowed red in the evening light. The two faced each other.

Fear snaked around Mark's heart.

The wolf moved its black head slowly from side to side, stretched its front legs, and lay back down on the stones, intent on Mark's face.

Mark stayed where he was, not taking his eyes off the wolf. The cold pebbles dug into his knees. From the corner of his eye he spied a second, and a third wolf. Their backs were to him, their muzzles raised to the air, ears alert. From somewhere distant came a long howl. A grey wolf rose to its haunches, lifted its head and howled an answer.

All three wolves rose, slowly ... like they didn't want him to be afraid, Mark thought, as much in hope as in certainty.

The black one who had been lying close to Mark nuzzled his arm. Mark went rigid. The wolf peered into his eyes and, to Mark's astonishment, gently wagged its tail.

Like a friendly dog.

An image came to him, of Verian standing in front of the red-tinted rock wall with her hands entwined in the black fur of a wolf.

Verian. This must be Verian's wolf.

'Are you helping me?'

The black wolf blinked its red eyes. The two which had been scanning the trees walked steadily up the stony bank and into the forest. The black wolf nuzzled Mark's arm again, loped towards the trees, came back to nudge Mark once more, vigorously, and ran after its fellows.

Go with them?

Mark clambered to his feet and squelched up the bank in his wet boots.

***

The summer dawn came early, and with it came red-haired Isa. She untied Gwen from the tree and pulled her, stumbling with her bound hands and cold, stiff legs, to the rekindled fire. The fat Madach, Manny, and his stringy-haired brother Viv stood there, silent and morose. Leather bundles were tied to their backs, long knives hung from their belts and each carried a stout pole.

'Will she be all right?' Isa asked Manny.

'What kinda question is that?'

Viv took the rope from Isa, and with no word to anyone jostled Gwen out of the camp. Manny stomped along behind.

'You'll see!'

Gwen strained over her shoulder. The solid Madach with long, greying blonde hair stood outside his tent, shaking his fist.

Why did this Madach so desperately want to tell the unknown

74

woman about Gwen? Why did the woman want her?

For no good reason. Although it might be better than being sold as a slave. Gwen's stomach roiled.

Viv pulled Gwen quickly along a narrow track. Tree roots constantly threatened to trip her and it was hard to think of anything except trying to stay on her feet. Her sick feeling grew worse, her legs were sore from the ropes and from being bent uncomfortably all through the night. Her back ached.

Through the pain and soreness, two questions pawed at Gwen's mind like a hungry beast. Would she ever see the Forest again? And if she did, how would she tell her mother about Mark?

For a long time, with no food, thirsty, Gwen was hustled along. At last, when the sun was about halfway to its highest point, the Madach halted.

'Good place for a break.' Manny slumped onto a fallen log. 'Should be there by this evening if our likely buyers ain't moved camp. Do our business and afterwards go on to see what else we can find.' He chuckled. 'Like more Danae wandering about. On our way to the ocean.'

Gwen glowered at him.

Both Madach threw their bundles to the ground. Manny took hold of Gwen's rope and Viv moved off the track, into the trees.

Gwen closed her eyes, feeling the sun warm her face. She was very tired. If she could lie down and sleep, forget for a time about Sleih and Madach kidnappers and being sold to the highest bidder ... how lovely it would be.

And grieve for Mark, properly.

A scream split the air.

Gwen's eyes shot open.

Another scream.

Manny's head jerked up.

Birds shrieked and fled the trees with a raucous rustling of leaves and wings.

The shrill screams kept coming.

'Help!'

Something scrabbled in the bushes. Gwen's heart jumped at the snap of breaking branches.

'Help!'

Manny pulled out his knife. The rope holding Gwen fell from his hands.

Viv burst onto the path, stringy hair streaming behind him.

'Wolves! Help! Run! Run!'

His long legs carried him swiftly back down the path, screaming.

Gwen's throat went dry. Wolves! She must flee too, she must run.

Her legs refused to move.

Manny stared after Viv's fleeing back. He glanced at Gwen, saw the dropped rope, and dived to the ground to retrieve it.

Gwen, her mind on escape, from the wolves, from the Madach, twisted to tug the rope out of reach.

Manny groped desperately in the dirt. He gave up on the rope and lunged for Gwen. She jumped away from him – and opened her mouth in horror.

Three long wolves, red eyes glinting, white teeth bared, catapulted out of the forest. One streaked after the fleeing Viv. Two sprang at fat Manny.

'Wolves! Run!' Manny tore down the path behind his brother.

The wolves flew after him.

Gwen's knees trembled. Her legs refused to move.

Run! she begged herself.

The Madach's screams shrilled in her ears.

Run!

'Gwen, Gwen!'

What?

Gwen whirled around.

'Mark?'

'Here, I'm here.'

And there he was, scrambling out from the trees where the wolves had been, grinning.

His hair was more tousled than usual, with bits of leaves and bark caught here and there, and his cloak was filthy and ripped in places where it hadn't been ripped before.

But he was alive.

'You're not drowned?'

'Appears not.' Mark spun about on his toes to show how not drowned he was.

Forgetting her bound hands, Gwen tried to hug him and nearly toppled them both to the ground.

Gwen stared. 'How?'

'It was the wolves, Verian's wolves, or at least I think they must be Verian's wolves, or their neighbours, or something.' Mark waved his arms. 'One pulled me from the river, right before the falls – you should see those falls, Gwen, massive, I wouldn't have survived them, not at all.' He paused, shrugged. 'The wolves saved me, pulled me out.'

Gwen sought to take it all in. 'The wolves, those wolves?' She gestured with her head down the path where the Madach's screams had faded. 'They're with you?'

'Uh huh. Though I suppose I'm with the wolves really.' Mark laughed.

'How did you find me?'

'I didn't, the wolves did. They led me here, all through the night. We've been tracking you and those two for ages.' He puffed his chest out. 'I must be a good tracker, eh, 'cos none of you had any clue I was there.'

'Can you untie me? There.' Gwen tilted her head to where the Madach had dropped his knife. 'Use the knife.'

Mark delicately sliced through the ropes.

'It's so good to see you!' Gwen hugged her brother with her freed arms until he squirmed out of her arms, blushing. 'Now let's get out of here before those Madach come back.'

Or the wolves.

'Yes, let's. And look at this.' Mark picked up the leather bundles discarded in the grass. He handed one to Gwen. 'What a pity, those Madach forgot to take these with them.'

They slung the heavy bundles over their shoulders and hurried away, further from the Madach camp.

Chapter Fifteen

Josh

'I'd love to catch that rabbit and roast it for supper.'

Mark was tired, his feet hurt, and he was hungry. The robbers' food was down to its last handful of hard bread. They were living off what they could find in the forest and Mark was sick of berries and nettle soup.

They also couldn't tell if they were any closer to the mythical Sleih. They hadn't stayed long on the path the robbers had been taking with Gwen, fearful of where, or rather to whom, it might lead. They found a faint, ancient way westward, marked from time to time with spilled piles of stones, and had followed it for two days. On the third day it disappeared under grass and bushes, the stone markers scattered on the forest floor.

The rabbit Mark wanted to roast had poked its head out to stare at them a few times.

'I'm sure it's the same rabbit.'

Gwen sniffed. 'It can't be the same rabbit. It's, well, all rabbits look the same.'

'It is absolutely the same rabbit. In fact, I think it's following us.'

'Don't be stupid.'

'I'm not being stupid.'

Mark groaned as rain began to fall. He pulled the hood of his cloak over his head with a sharp tug. It was a brief summer storm shower, heavy enough to dampen his clothes through his tattered cloak and make him shiver in the chill air. The shower passed, the clouds breaking apart to reveal a brilliant red sunset directly ahead.

'There you are!' Mark pointed at the setting sun. 'I said this way was west.'

'Yes, you did, after I persuaded you not to go in the completely opposite direction.'

'Do you mean along a path which seemed it might actually be used by something other than deer?'

'Yes, the well-used path. The Beings only know where we'd be if we'd taken it. Probably in a robber Madach camp. Far to the east.'

'Or having supper with the Sleih.'

Gwen humphed and marched on. Mark stomped behind, scowling.

'Shall we find somewhere to camp for the night,' Gwen said, 'or do you want to go on while we know we're going in the right direction?'

'Don't care, as long as we have something more to eat tonight than last night.'

'No, what we eat tonight, we can't eat tomorrow.'

'Such wisdom, big sister.'

Gwen raised a hand to cuff him, when Mark said, 'There's the rabbit! It really does want to be eaten!'

The rabbit squatted squarely in their way, facing them, ears up like soldiers on parade.

'Let's catch it,' Mark whispered. 'We can decide if we're hungry enough to kill it and eat it once we've caught it.'

'If you can.'

Mark strolled nonchalantly towards the rabbit, pretending he hadn't seen it. The rabbit was unmoved. Mark pounced. The rabbit skipped nimbly to one side, took a few hops, and stopped.

'Strange,' Gwen said.

Mark pounced again. The rabbit skipped to one side.

'Playing, hey?' Mark said to the rabbit. To Gwen he said, 'A challenge. Bunny or me!'

Gwen giggled. 'I bet the bunny wins. And I couldn't eat it, not now. It's cheered me up too much.'

The rabbit regarded them with its head on one side before turning and hopping languidly ahead. It disappeared into a patch of longer grass. Gwen and Mark followed. There was the rabbit, preening its ears as if it had been patiently waiting for them.

Mark scratched his head. 'Umm, you don't think it wants us to go with it, do you?'

Gwen raised her eyebrows.

'Let's follow it, see what happens,' Mark said.

'Still intending to eat it?'

'Depends where it leads us.'

The rabbit seemed to understand. It hopped a short way down the narrow trail. It looked back at them.

Mark grinned. 'There, you see, it wants to make sure we're coming too.'

And then they were chasing after the rabbit, through flower-filled clearings, down a path, along another, beside a stream and over a rough ford of uneven stones. When the rabbit went straight through a patch of nettles, Mark and Gwen had to skirt around to avoid being stung. And there was the rabbit, waiting for them, ears down. It immediately pricked its ears, taking off between the trees. They had to keep close, to make sure they didn't lose the rabbit in the deepening shadows.

Night was well on its way when the rabbit hopped into a small forest of bracken. Mark and Gwen pushed through after it, and pulled up short, panting from their efforts.

'Oh,' Gwen said.

Mark realised he wasn't at all surprised to find himself in a clearing where a small fire was about to bloom into a proper blaze. The clearing was sheltered by an oak with a girth the size of a cottage towering against a grassy bank. The oak's roots stood as tall as Mark. Washing hung from a low branch. Chickens scratched around beneath the washing.

'The rabbit couldn't have led us to a robber camp, could it?' Gwen said. She held on to Mark's arm to stop him going any further.

'Do you think we should hide and see who lives here?' he said.

'Too late.'

Mark followed Gwen's pointing finger to where a very strange person was emerging from between the roots of the oak.

***

'Who's this, eh? Visitors? If I'd known I would have tidied up, ha ha!'

Gwen was sure the speaker was a Danae. Whether he was or not, he was extremely old, much older than anyone she knew in the villages. His skinny shoulders were hunched to ears which stuck out below an untidy ponytail of white hair. He wore badly patched trousers held up by a belt of plaited ivy, no shoes, and a threadbare shirt of a long forgotten colour. In his hands he carried a dented pot.

'Good thing I made a big pot of supper tonight.' Brown eyes sparkled at Gwen from under heavy, white brows. 'Assume you're hungry? My experience is, children are always hungry. Although not many children here now. In fact, no children. Actually, no one 'cept me here.'

As the old Danae sounded cheerful about this, Gwen didn't think she needed to feel sad for him.

'Sit down, sit down, take the weight off your feet.' He nodded at a log set near the fire, with a pile of wood handy to anyone who might sit on the log. He placed the dented pot at the edge of the blaze, covered it with a dented lid and sat back on his heels.

'Won't take long to cook. A few vegetables, late spring mushrooms, bit of wild garlic to give it a good flavour.'

At the mention of wild garlic, Gwen's thoughts flew to Lucy. She shivered.

The old man inspected them both. 'Bit damp. Got caught in the rain, did you?'

'Yes,' Mark said. 'The rabbit. Did it lead us here?'

The old man raised his eyebrows. 'Didn't he tell you where he was bringing you?'

Gwen laughed. 'Well, no, we're not properly fluent in Rabbit,' she said. 'It did seem to know where it was going though.'

'Of course he did. He told me about you two a couple of days back, and I said to myself, well they sound like Danae children, not Sleih or Madach, and maybe they're lost and maybe they're looking for something or someone or somewhere, and maybe old Josh should help them out. If he can. Besides, haven't had any Danae company for a long time.' He looked from one to the other. 'You are Danae, eh?'

'Yes.' Mark had apparently forgotten they weren't to tell anyone this. 'I'm Mark, this is my sister, Gwen.'

The old man nodded. 'The creatures are fine, but there's nothing like your own kind for a good natter and a gossip is there, eh?'

Gwen wasn't sure what to make of this although she found she wasn't alarmed by Mark giving them away this easily.

'No, there isn't,' she said.

At Josh's invitation, she and Mark rested on the log, waiting for the supper to cook while the fire dried out their clothes.

***

They ate the supper – served in wooden bowls which had seen many suppers – in silence except for the occasional slurp. Mark finally patted his stomach. 'I couldn't eat another mouthful.'

All three of them settled against the log and stretched their feet to the glowing coals.

Darkness had arrived. The clouds had cleared and the stars were plentiful. The moon was waxing and would be full in a day or two. The forest was quiet except for the occasional scuffling noise from a small night animal or the flutter of wings from a hunting bird.

Gwen asked the first of many questions on her mind.

'How long is it since you had a natter and a gossip with other Danae?'

'Why, must have been with Gillian. Gone now, buried over there, with the others.' Josh pointed into the darkness to a place beyond the oak. 'Long time ago. I'm the last.'

He must be lonely, Gwen thought.

'Not lonely, no.' Josh shook his head at Gwen. 'I have the animals and I keep busy with different things, and in the winter I have my books. Not lonely, no.'

Gwen shifted her head sharply. 'You know what I'm thinking?'

Josh glanced sideways at her. 'I can't actually read your mind, just tell pretty much what you're feeling and thinking, like with the wild creatures.'

'The wild creatures?' Mark said. 'You mean you really did know the rabbit had seen us?'

'You can understand the creatures, and us?' Gwen's eyes were wide.

Josh's own eyes widened. 'You're sure you're Danae?' he said, with the merest hint of humour.

'Yes,' Mark said. 'We're Danae from the Forest, by the edge of the sea.'

'Yet you can't hear each other, or the wild things?'

'Are we supposed to?'

Josh's brow furrowed. 'What do you know about the Danae before they came to the Forest?'

'We know,' Gwen said, 'that the Madach wanted our lands and houses and all the good things we had in The Place Before, and they drove us out. And the Sleih helped us, or at least the legends say they did.'

'The Sleih helped you? Is that what they say? Mmm, interesting.'

Now Gwen asked the most important question. 'You mentioned the Sleih before, saying we weren't Sleih, or Madach. Do you mean the Sleih exist?'

'Yes, of course, absolutely the Sleih exist.'

A relieved smile spread over Gwen's face.

'Always have to my knowledge,' Josh said, 'like there's always been Madach.' He paused. 'Haven't always been Danae.'

Mark had been smiling at Gwen, nodding. The smile somersaulted into a scowl. 'What do you mean, haven't always been Danae?'

Josh sighed. 'Appears there's a lot you don't know about your own people.' He wriggled to settle more comfortably. 'Would you like to hear the story of the Danae?'

'Yes,' Mark said.

'And of the Sleih too, please,' Gwen said.

'All one story.'

A fox lay spread like an old dog at Josh's feet. He absently stroked its brushy tail. 'The story of the Sleih, the Madach and the Danae,' Josh said.

Chapter Sixteen

The Sleih, The Madach And The Danae

'Once upon a time,' Josh began in a sing-song, story-telling voice, like he'd told the story many times, 'in a land not far from here, the Madach and the Sleih lived in harmony – well, almost. The Sleih lived in a beautiful city, the Citadel of Ilatias, with streets paved with gold (they say) and houses built of marble and exotic stones and richly patterned woods. The windows were made of diamonds, and the furnishings in the houses were decorated with elaborate carvings painted with gold and inset with jewels of all kinds.'

This sounded more like the kind of Sleih Gwen imagined. She nodded.

'The Sleih wore silks and furs and fine linens.' Josh ran his hands down his skinny arms to show the soft luxuriousness of the Sleih clothes. 'And they covered their arms and necks with beautiful jewellery.' He stroked the backs of his hands up his scrawny neck and grinned at Gwen. 'Their ruler was a wise king. He'd been their ruler for many years, because the Sleih live for a long, long time.'

Josh squinted at Mark. 'Do you know why the Sleih live for a long, long time?'

'No.'

'The magic in them,' Josh said. 'As long as they use the magic. They have to believe in the magic and use it all the time. The more they use the magic, the longer they live.'

Magic? Gwen was suddenly cautious of this story of the Danae and the fine Sleih.

Josh gave her a wry look. 'I know it sounds like a baby's bedtime tale, except it's true. I'm not totally sure about the diamond windows and the gold-paved streets. It's certainly true about the magic.'

Gwen decided to enjoy the story anyway. She wanted to hear about the Danae. And the Sleih.

Mark's gaze was fixed on the old man. 'Go on.'

Josh poked at the fire with a stick. 'The Madach owned the land around the Citadel. Do to this day, far as I know. They worked it and were prosperous, and they lived in comfortable houses and built villages with schools and inns and market squares. They traded with the Sleih, bringing their goods into the Citadel to sell for gold and jewels which they used to buy seed and cattle from Madach in places far away. Their lands went right down to the sea, and there they built wharves and docks and traded goods from all over the world.

'Of course, there were problems from time to time, and sometimes a group of Madach (never the Sleih) would sail off in search of other lands. Most of 'em never came back, so I suppose they found somewhere better to live. Or drowned. But all in all, the two peoples got along well together.'

Josh peered closely at Gwen. 'With me so far?'

'Yes.'

'Sometimes,' Josh said, 'a Sleih would marry a Madach, or a Madach would marry a Sleih. Both peoples were happy with this. At least, they were until the children arrived.' He sighed. 'The children didn't inherit the best of either side I'm afraid. Most had a little magic, from the Sleih side. They had some gift for hearing their brothers and sisters without speech and many had the gift of listening to the wild creatures. That was it, though. Nothing like the magic of their Sleih parents. Neither did they have the size and physical strength of their Madach

87

parents. The poor children. They weren't much welcome by either kind and over time – because the marriages kept on happening and the children grew up and had their own children – over time they came together in their own community.'

Gwen was waiting for the Danae to be mentioned when Mark said, staring at Josh, 'You know what we're thinking, and the animals too. You have some magic powers like the Sleih, yet you're Danae.' His voice grew louder. 'Are we partly Sleih? Do we have magic too?'

'Ah, you are clever!' Josh beamed at his new student. 'Yes, you're right. You're half Sleih.'

Oh! Gwen understood. And yes, they might be half Sleih, but they were also half Madach. Gwen grimaced.

'No doubt you have some magic in you,' Josh said, 'although if neither of you can hear each other or the wild creatures, seems it's buried deeply in your people by now.' He frowned. 'Do you know any of your Danae who've got any kind of gifts?'

'Hmm,' Gwen said softly. She faced Mark. 'Callie's strange sometimes, with her nightmares and her ... well, I suppose they're sort of trances, like Verian.'

'Verian, of course,' Mark said. 'She's friendly with the wolves and sees things others can't. And she's Danae, at least we think she's Danae.'

'I don't think Callie can talk to animals,' Gwen said. 'Although she does love them.'

Josh didn't ask who Callie or Verian were. Gwen was about to tell him when Mark said, 'Go on. What happened next?'

Josh wriggled against the log. The fox briefly lifted its head and settled back at Josh's feet.

'So we have the three peoples living together, unfortunately not in harmony any more. The Madach are tall and big and strong, and they didn't like to see the small Danae, knowing their blood flowed in their bodies. The Sleih too, proud of their magic powers, were rather ashamed of these people with their weaker magic and didn't like having them around either. The poor Danae weren't welcome to work in the fields with the Madach and they weren't welcome in the Citadel either.'

Gwen grew indignant on her ancestors' behalf. How dare these Sleih and Madach consider her people inferior. At least the Danae weren't evil like the Madach.

It came to a head one year, Josh told them, when a group of young Danae decided to fight for their rights – Gwen nodded approvingly – wanting to work land from their Madach forefathers or to live in the Citadel studying magic with their Sleih grandmothers, although they generally made poor students. They caused a lot of trouble, storming into magic classes and refusing to leave, or gathering in fields to stop the Madach farmers ploughing or harvesting.

'The Madach and the Sleih ended up agreeing the kindest thing, for themselves anyway,' Josh said, 'would be to move this troublesome people on, to a new land where they could do what they wanted without bothering the Madach and the Sleih.' He paused, absently patted the fox's velvety head. 'You know the rest. They drove us out, into the Forest, and here we live to this day.'

It seemed Josh had finished the story.

'Don't know where you all got this notion the Sleih helped us,' he grumbled. 'They were as much to blame as the Madach.'

Silvery curls and a broken wheel passed through Gwen's mind. Sorrow added itself to her indignation. All the fault of the Madach and, it seemed, the Sleih too.

'In fact, worse,' Josh said under his breath.

'Worse?'

'The Sleih, graciously'–Josh's tone was sarcastic–'did give the Danae a few provisions, no doubt to make sure we got far enough away so we didn't all die too close to home. Probably where your people got the idea of help from. But they wanted a price for their selfish bit of help.' Josh prodded the fire with the stick. A small volcano of red embers billowed into the night.

He was silent so long Gwen was worried he wouldn't say anymore.

'What was the price?' she said.

'A very high one.' Josh sighed a deep, sad sigh of loss. 'They kept behind one child from each family. Can you imagine?' His voice rose in indignation to match Gwen's. 'Forced out of your home, and have to leave a child behind as well? Some help the Sleih gave, eh?'

Gwen thought of her mother's grief over Lucy. Tears pricked her eyelids.

'Why did the Sleih do that? What happened to the children?' Mark said.

'Don't know why they were kept behind, don't know what happened to them. Terrible business, terrible. It was the youngest ones had to be left behind, the younger the better, even babies. Caused a lot of sadness.' Josh gazed into the flames.

Gwen had a new thought. 'Josh, were you one of the Danae who left The Place Before? Are you so old? Did your family have to leave a child behind?'

'Yes.'

Josh kept his eyes on the fire.

'Clara. Sweet baby, she was.'

He roused himself. 'All a long, long time ago.' He stood up. The fox flicked its tail at the disturbance, otherwise unmoved. 'And now it's time for sleep. Lots to do tomorrow, got to get you two sorted, work out what you have to do.'

'We haven't told you why we're here,' Mark said. 'Or do you know already?'

'No, no. I can see you've been travelling through the Forest for some time. Not much magic there, just need to see the state of you both. And I can tell you're searching for someone, it's clear in your minds. Tell me in the morning. Too late tonight. Need to sleep.'

He led them to the oak, holding a lantern lit by a coal from the fire.

'In here, should be blankets. Might be a pillow or two.' He pointed them to one of the many room-like spaces which led from the entrance into the depths of the grassy bank. Leaving the lantern, he wandered off to another part of the great roots of the tree.

Chapter Seventeen

A Gift Of Silver

Mark was into his second breakfast helping of egg and mushrooms when Josh said, 'So why are you two wandering, lost, in the Deep Forest?'

Gwen leaned back against the log by the fire, her plate on her lap.

'Our villages are a long way from here,' she said, 'right at the edge of the Forest, by the sea. We look after ourselves, have nothing to do with anyone else, ever.'

Mark waved his tarnished fork in the air. 'Except,' he said, 'when the Madach come sometimes in a ship and stop for water, or wood for repairs. We make sure they don't see us.'

'The last time they came,' Gwen said, 'they came in two ships and they didn't leave.'

'And,' Mark said, 'they discovered the villages, which is why Gwen and me had to run away before they could stop us. We're supposed to find the Sleih, to ask for their help to get these Madach to go back where they came from.'

Mark put his plate on the ground and looked at Josh. The old Danae perched on the log with a hand on each knee, gazing into the trees.

'The Danae risk being thrown out of their homes by the Madach for a second time, eh?'

'Yes.'

'Why do you think the Sleih will help?'

'We don't know if they will,' Gwen said. 'Especially after what you told us last night. There's no one else to ask.' She put her own plate on the ground. 'We think the Sleih may have taken our sister, Lucy. She was picking wild garlic in the Forest and never came home. We know there was a horse, and the horse went west.'

'Mmm,' Josh said. 'Well, if she's there, she's likely safe and well. The Sleih aren't cruel you know, only strange.'

'We just hope Madach kidnappers haven't caught her and sold her, like they wanted to do with us,' Mark said.

Josh narrowed his eyes. 'Had a run-in with Madach robbers?'

'Gwen did. I fell out of the boat and would have drowned 'cept for a wolf hauling me out, and the wolves and me saved Gwen.'

Josh raised his eyebrows.

'I think the wolves who saved us came from Verian,' Mark said.

'Verian?'

'Before we were caught by the Madach, we found other Danae,' Gwen said.

'Other Danae? Really? Wasn't it wonderful to find other Danae? Didn't they want to help you?'

'Sort of, although not in any useful way.'

Gwen told the story of the strange queen and her mad plan to make the Danae live underground, and about Verian's trance-like sayings, sayings which kept whirling around and around in her head: *the hissing monster, fear searing her mind, the market sellers' calls ... a fairytale, a fairytale ...*

Finally, she told Josh about the argument in the Madach camp, about the woman who wanted to find the Danae children travelling through the forest, and not for any good reason, Gwen suspected.

Josh sat on the log, listening. At the end, he whooshed out a breath. 'Well, what a tale.'

'We have to be careful,' Gwen said, 'not to let people know we're Danae. At least until we find the Sleih.'

Josh said nothing more about wolves or queens. He stood up from the log, whistled into the trees, and sat down again.

'The day's getting on,' he said. 'We better set you on your way, no time to lose.'

The fox who had lain at Josh's feet by the fire trotted into the clearing. He had a handsome fox friend with him.

'Now you two,' Josh said, 'I have a job which I know you'll love. How about a trip to the Madach farms?'

The foxes lifted their black lips in foxy grins.

'I want you to lead these two as far as the road to the Citadel. Keep them safe from robber Madach, make sure they reach the road and know where to go. Will you take them?'

The foxes trotted to the edge of the clearing, brushy tails erect.

'Hey, slow down,' Josh said. 'Danae have to take a few supplies when we go on journeys, not like you animals.'

They spent the rest of the morning putting together what food Josh could find for them and learning about some unfamiliar plants which bore berries and fruits they could eat. 'You won't go hungry with these. Plenty of 'em about this time of year.'

Eventually, they were ready. They were about to say farewell when Josh mumbled to himself and darted back under the oak.

Several minutes went by. Gwen began to believe Josh simply didn't want to say goodbye, and they should leave, when he ran back out.

He handed a small cloth bag to Gwen. 'Something in there which might help you. Maybe.'

'What is it?' Mark said.

Gwen carefully untied the threadbare ribbon around the bag, reached inside and drew out a delicate silver chain.

Silver.

Gwen heard Verian's warning. I see you with silver. I cannot see if it is for ill or for good. And Josh's doubtful ... might help you. Maybe.

A small and intricate pendant was attached to the silver chain. It was shaped like a strange bird, of a kind Gwen had never seen before. The tiny blue head was fashioned as an eagle, while the silver body, with its curled and tufted tail, reminded her of an over-sized white cat. The bird-like creature lay on its side in repose, one dark blue wing rising up behind, the other closed against its side.

'It's beautiful.' Gwen turned the pendant over. 'What is it? And how can it help us?'

Or hurt?

'A gryphon,' Josh said. 'Don't suppose you know what a gryphon is, do you?'

Gwen shook her head.

'It's a mythical beast which the stories say lived among the Sleih, oh, a long, long time ago. The pendant'–he reached out a long, thin finger to the jewelled gryphon–'came from my Sleih great-great-grandmamma. Family legend says it's a charm to ward off evil, or guard the wearer from danger or bad magic.'

He spread his arms out wide, shrugged. 'Never saw anyone use it, and it didn't ward off those Madach who sent us into the Forest, did it?'

The pendant lay lightly on Gwen's palm. Help or danger – either way, she knew she couldn't give it up. Still, she said, 'Are you sure you want to give it away, Josh? Isn't it precious to you?'

'No, not precious to me, not at all. Forgotten all about it until now, when I thought, the charm, must give them the charm. Might help, never know.'

This was enough for Gwen. 'Thank you, and I promise to take care of it, and to bring it back when all this is over.'

Josh grinned. 'You do that.'

Gwen lifted the thin chain, reached behind her head and fastened the clasp. She gave the chain a gentle tug to make sure it was secure. The gryphon nestled into the hollow at the base of her neck.

At last they were ready to move. The foxes, bored with all the Danae preparations, had gone to sleep by the fire and had to be roused. They sprang up immediately, ears and tails pricked.

'Time to be off! Make sure they're safe, eh?' Josh said, wagging a finger.

Gwen thanked Josh for everything he'd done. Mark promised to come back when all was safe with the Danae. Josh appeared pleased despite grumbling about visitors eating him out of house and home. Gwen kissed him on his rough wrinkled cheek. Mark shook Josh's hand.

Waving, Gwen and Mark followed the foxes' brushy tails out of the clearing, heading west.

Chapter Eighteen

The Place Before

The foxes proved good guides, searching out trails wide enough for human feet, stopping each evening where a stream and a rocky overhang or a shallow cave in a hillside made a comfortable, dry place to camp. Gwen started noticing the trees were not the giants they'd become used to. They also seemed more obliging, no longer swapping places with their neighbours during the night or coiling their roots around skinny ankles. The night noises softened, became more the hoots and hushed calls and quick patter of skittering animals Gwen knew from her own Forest.

Late one hot afternoon when bulbous clouds were thickening above them, they came to a broad track through the trees. The foxes led Mark and Gwen onto its smooth surface, glancing in all directions before cautiously trotting northwards. They'd not gone far when Gwen spotted a traveller heading their way. He was pushing a small barrow. The foxes crept into the undergrowth.

'Should we hide?' Gwen said.

'We can't hide forever, and he doesn't seem to be a robber or a kidnapper, does he?'

Gwen kept her head down, hoping their unfamiliarity with this strange land didn't scream out loud. The barrowman glanced up at the sky, said, 'Afternoon. Bit of a storm coming, eh?' and passed on by.

Gwen breathed out loudly. Her heart thumped, and her hands were damp.

The foxes crawled out from the ferns by the wayside only to slink back in when a second traveller approached. He was a labourer with a bunch of tools over his shoulder, wearily making his way home. He barely lifted his head as they passed. When the foxes came back, they kept close to the side of the track, ears alert.

The afternoon grew late. The trees on either side thinned, and finally ceased altogether.

Gwen stopped, eyes widening as she gazed out at a world she could never have imagined. A plain of fields criss-crossed with hedges and wooden fences stretched endlessly before her. Wheat and corn and potatoes grew high and lush in many of the fields. Fat white sheep and hefty brown cows grazed in others, along with sturdy horses. Scattered in the fields were farm houses and outbuildings, built of a sandy-coloured stone or wide white-painted timbers, all with red roofs. Smoke from evening fires curled into the warm, windless air.

Mark also stared at this unfamiliar land.

'It's so, so, well, open,' he said.

Gwen's eyes roamed from one distant horizon to another. The sky was huge. She found herself reluctant to go forward.

'It'd be difficult to hide here, if we need to,' she said.

'Yes. Let's hope we don't have to.'

Gwen jumped as one of the foxes brushed against her. She glanced down into a pair of amber eyes.

'You want to get off this road, don't you?' The amber eyes blinked.

'We keep going up there, I suppose?' Gwen pointed straight ahead, along the track, northwards. The fox blinked.

Gwen nodded. 'Thank you for bringing us this far.'

Both foxes gave a flick of their tails, a goodbye wave, and slunk into the grass.

Gwen stared wistfully at the place where the foxes had disappeared. She felt lonely and lost without their confident company. She wanted to be home in her Forest, not wandering in this unfamiliar, open land with no one to guide them. She sniffed the air. It smelled of warm grass. Not like a forest at all.

'Come on, let's get going.' Mark started forward. 'We need to find shelter before this storm breaks.'

Gwen hitched her bag over her shoulder and set off with determined steps.

'It'd be good to know how much further it is to the Citadel,' she said as Mark fell into step beside her. 'We don't have much food left either.'

Mark studied the fields. 'We could sleep in one of the farm buildings and see if there happens to be any sort of food lying about waiting to be eaten while we're there.'

'Steal, you mean?'

'Well, it's stealing from the Madach and they stole it all from us in the first place.'

'Mmm.' Gwen paused. 'Do you think we're there, in The Place Before?'

'Could be.'

They walked on. To their left the sun was dipping below the horizon, colouring the thickening clouds with gold, reds and oranges. The air was hot, damp and breathless.

A cart piled high with hay and pulled by two huge horses clopped past them. The Madach driver's head was on his chest, the reins lying loosely on his lap. He gave no sign of seeing Gwen and Mark, although the nearest horse swung its massive head towards them and snickered softly.

The storm burst just as the sun gave in for the day. The clouds broke, deluging them with heavy, cold drops of rain.

'Down here.' Mark scurried along a farm track to a barn.

They slid through the not-quite-closed barn door into

a clutter of carts and farm tools and sacks of grain. A pile of rough bags offered a welcome cosiness from the cooling evening air, and they made themselves comfortable as they shared the last of Josh's provisions.

'What are we going to do when we reach the Citadel?' Mark said, hunting in his bag to see if there was anything at all to eat.

'I suppose it all depends on how welcoming these Sleih are.'

'Do you think we'll be allowed to see the king of the Sleih?'

'I don't know.'

Gwen worried about Josh's story that the Sleih also wanted to be rid of the Danae. Josh had told them the king who ruled when the Danae were thrown out had died at a great old age. Gwen hoped whichever king ruled now would be more sympathetic to the Danae than his forebears had been.

'If Josh is right, the king might send us packing,' she said. 'If we get to speak to him at all.'

'King or not,' Mark said, half-asleep, 'we have to find Lucy too.'

***

They woke before dawn and crept from the barn, silently helping themselves to a raw breakfast of peas and beans from a vegetable patch hidden from the farmhouse by a wooden fence.

A black dog watched them through a gap in the fence. Gwen waited for the dog to give the alarm. The dog wagged its tail and trotted back to the farmhouse.

They were back on the road as the sun went up.

Lots of laden carts were also heading north and Gwen was uncomfortable about the many curious glances she and Mark received. She hoped it was because they were children on their own, not because they didn't appear to be Madach.

Or possibly, she considered, eyeing Mark's cloak as he walked steadily beside her, because they were ragged and dirty.

No one challenged them, however.

***

'I wish we knew how far it is to the Citadel.'

Gwen paddled her swollen feet in a stream which flowed beside the road, grateful for the shade of a chestnut tree. The sun beat down and the road was hot, and dusty with all the traffic. They'd refilled their water bottles and Gwen was trying not to think about the lack of lunch.

'We could ask someone,' Mark said.

'I'd rather not. These Madach don't seem too interested in us, though they might change their minds if they find out we're a long way from home and what we are.' Gwen pulled on her cracked boots, hoisted her bag. 'Let's keep going. The sooner we move, the sooner we'll be there.'

The countryside changed little. All around them were fields and gently rising hills scattered with red-roofed farmhouses and barns. Far to the north, Gwen could make out the shadowy shapes of lofty mountains, their tips touched with white.

They spent the night in another barn, their supper a handful of fat purple plums they plucked from a tree overhanging the road. Gwen slept fitfully, her stomach growling. She was glad to be up and on the road the next morning, for another day's walking.

Chapter Nineteen

Other Quests

High in the towers of the Citadel of Ilatias, sunlight streamed through the mottled glass windows of Lady Melda's solar. It picked out the dust motes floating above tables scattered with books, paper, inkwells and orbs, glasses, tubes and all the paraphernalia used by Seers of the Sleih.

Shelves, overflowing with more books and papers, lined the walls, except where a big map of the known world hung. Ilatias was at the centre of this map. North were the High Alps of Asfarlon, forever swathed in white. The far east, past the Madach fields and farms, was coloured green, and named Arneithe, the Deep Forest. To the west were more fields, with the names of the occasional town and village marked in neat, black lettering. South was coloured blue, for the oceans, stretching away to unfamiliar lands. Even here, countries, towns and cities were named, in the same neat, black lettering.

Lady Melda paced between the tables, hands clasped behind her back, brow furrowed. Anger bubbled through her like a fiery liquid. She'd visited every robber Madach camp she knew in the Deep Forest, asking about the Danae children. All she received were blank stares from what she considered gormless faces, and promises she didn't believe to send word if anyone heard or saw anything.

No word had come, none at all. It was as if these children didn't exist.

Were they dead? Lost, starved, in the Deep Forest of Arneithe?

If they were dead, it would make her part of the bargain simple. She'd promised the Madach conqueror, Lord Rafe, she would stop these Danae children from reaching the Sleih and asking for help against his men – those men who were claiming the forest for their master. If she succeeded and Rafe got his forest and his Danae fairytale slaves, he would have to fulfil his part of the bargain – delivering Ilatias into her hands.

Lady Melda pushed her anger aside to gaze dreamily at the centre of the big map. She humphed, and went back to the frustrating question of where these Danae could be.

They couldn't be dead.

Danae, from a primitive village at the edge of nowhere, must surely be capable of surviving in the Deep Forest.

She paced some more, her anger flaring.

Anyway, she must know for certain. There was too much to lose if it all went wrong.

She stopped pacing.

'Ratty, I have an errand for you.'

The rat stood on its hind legs and blinked at her from its customary spot on the window sill, surrounded by gnawed bones.

Errand? How far? It's hot out there.

Lady Melda raised her eyebrows. 'It'll be cooler where I'm sending you.'

The rat dropped its front paws to the sill. *Well?*

'I need to find these Danae children before they reach the Citadel, before they talk to our weak-willed king and make their pleas for rescue from the wicked Madach.'

She strode to the window and picked the rat up by its scruff. She stared into its eyes.

'What I want you to do, my dear ratty, is to go into the Deep Forest and talk to your friends, see what they know about these children.'

The rat stared back, coolly.

'Especially,' Lady Melda's voice rose to a shout, 'where are they?'

The rat drew in its head as Lady Melda dropped it to the floor – her usual means of letting it go when she was in a rage.

Thud! The rat scuttled into a crack in the wall, tail flicking.

'And don't come back until you find them!'

***

Manny and Viv were tired of being made fun of.

'Wolves? And not a scratch on either of you?'

'Just say it, she escaped, didn't she? Scrap of a girl, besting two great men like you.'

Chester didn't do any teasing. He joined Manny and Viv where they sulked by the fire. Isa sat with them. All four stared glumly into the flames.

'What do you think this Blue Lady,' Chester gave Isa a sideways glance, 'will do to us, if she ever finds out, eh?'

Viv scratched his nose. 'Finds out what?'

'Finds out we had her Danae brats and we let one drown and the other escape.'

Manny shrugged.

'You weren't here when she came,' Chester said, not for the first time. 'Powerful, weren't she, eh, Isa?'

Isa bobbed her head vehemently. 'Her eyes, they're the worst bit. Make you feel like she can see right through you, know your every thought.'

'We should try and find her,' said Chester to the flames.

'Find who?' Manny said.

'Oh, the Blue Lady, of course! Who d'you think, you idiot? The girl, the girl, we gotta find the girl.'

'The girl? Where d'you suppose we might start looking, eh?'

Chester peered at Manny, who stared back with his squinty gaze.

'You and Viv,' Chester said, slowly, 'you should do what you were gonna do, go east, to the ocean, and find the rest of 'em. See if you can find the girl on your way. Even if you don't find her, when you come back we'll have enough Danae to spare for us and this lady, supposing she don't much care what Danae children she has.'

'You're right, Chester. Good thinking.' Manny held his fat-cheeked head higher. 'That'll show them all how brave and tough me and Viv is.'

'What if she's not heading home?' Viv said. 'What if she and the boy were going the other way?'

'Mmm,' Chester said. 'Think I'll move this lot on, closer to the Citadel, and me and a couple of the others, we'll follow the road, search for her in the villages. I mean, she can't survive here in the forest by herself for long, can she?'

'Unless the wolves already ate her,' Isa said. Her lips quivered.

The four of them stared into the fire.

***

The rat stood on its hind legs, scanning the crowd of its many relatives. Dank water dripped down the slime-smeared walls of the sewer drains. The rat slowly savoured the smell of home.

'Listen all of you. This is extremely important,' it said. The ends of its whiskers flicked pompously. 'A command from my benefactor and mistress.'

The rats were interested. Previous commands, when fulfilled, had been well-rewarded by the rat's benefactor. Bones, with juicy chunks of rotting meat clinging to them, wheaty biscuits, and, best of all, chocolate.

'Children, Danae children, we have to find some,' the rat said.

'Danae? They're a fairytale,' a fat brown rat said. 'How are we supposed to find a fairytale?'

'Apparently not, according to my benefactor.'

'Where are they?'

'That's the point,' the rat said patiently. 'She wants to know where they are.'

'What do they look like?'

'We don't know.'

'Then how are we going to know if we find them?'

'They're Danae. They won't look like Sleih and they won't look like Madach.'

The rats grumbled.

'Chocolate, I promise you all the chocolate you can eat, all of you, if someone finds out where these children are.'

The grumbling stopped. There was a loud scampering, ratty claws scratching on the sewer bricks.

The rat was alone.

Chapter Twenty

Market Day

The sun was at its highest when Gwen and Mark arrived, hot and hungry, at a small village with a big market square. Gwen stood at the edge of the square, taking in the market traders shouting out their wares and the shoppers with laden baskets haggling over prices.

Mark sniffed, long and loudly. 'Yum, over there.' He pointed to a row of tables where people were being served bowls of soup and steaming pies and plates of roasted meats and fragrant vegetables.

Gwen sniffed too. 'It does smell delicious. We've nothing to trade though, and I think everyone's using money ... Oh no!' She squeezed Mark's arm.

'What?'

'The Madach from the robber gang, they're here.' Gwen lowered her head. 'They mustn't see me.'

'Where? Which ones?'

'Those two, at the table.' She jabbed a finger, holding her arm close to her body. 'I'm sure one of them is the Madach who wanted to tell some lady about me, when they were arguing at the camp.'

Gwen sneaked a look from under her brows, and met the Madach's eyes. He hesitated, then tapped his companion on the shoulder.

Gwen's heart pounded.

'I think they've seen you,' Mark said.

'Let's go!' Gwen grabbed Mark's hand and dragged him across the market place. The robbers jumped up from their table.

'Run!'

Mark tore free of Gwen and took off, deeper into the market. He called over his shoulder, 'Come on, hurry.'

And ran straight into a well-rounded stallholder carrying a tray of pies.

Mark was brought up short, the stallholder went 'Oomph', and the pies fell into the dirt. Mark's attempt to keep running was thwarted by a heavy hand clutching his shoulder.

'By the Beings,' the stallholder said, gazing down at his pie-spattered white apron. 'What's all the rush? My poor pies!'

'I'm sorry.' Gwen searched the market place while she apologised.

The robbers had disappeared.

'They were after us, the robbers were after us.' Mark, too, stared all around.

'Robbers?'

'Yes, they caught us once before and they still want us.'

'Really?' The stallholder's steady gaze wandered over their unkempt hair, their torn and dirty clothes. 'Robbers are after you?'

Gwen didn't know how to answer this. Instead she said, 'We're sorry about your pies and I'd give you money for them, except we don't have any, so all I can say is how sorry we are.'

The stallholder stroked his beardless, plump chin. 'Busy at the moment. Tell you what, you two wait here and when I'm done you can help me pack up the cart by way of paying for the pies. Okay?'

Gwen hesitated. She wanted to get out of the market, away from Madach robbers.

The stallholder seemed to read her mind. 'No robbers can

steal you from here,' he said. 'I'll be there'–he pointed to a stall laid out with all kinds of pies–'and if the people chasing you come near, scream.'

'Yes, thank you. We'll stay, because we do want to pay for the pies, somehow.'

'Good.'

The stallholder went back to his customers and Gwen sat on the ground next to the cart. Mark sat beside her, eyeing the remains of the pies.

Gwen raised her eyebrows. 'No, you're not going to eat dirty pie.'

The smells from the food stalls were hard to ignore and Gwen's stomach roiled with hunger. Just when she believed she couldn't sit there any longer, the stallholder came back to his cart, removed more pies and handed one each to Gwen and Mark. He rushed off before either could thank him.

Mark bit into his pie. 'Mmm.'

They waited more contentedly now, resting against the cart's high wheels, watching the bustling market. Gwen was almost asleep when the stallholder returned.

'Bit better now, with food inside you?'

'Thank you, yes, delicious,' Mark said.

'Good. Let's pack up this cart.'

Packing didn't take long, with very little left over. When they were done, Gwen was about to say thank you and move off, when the stallholder said, 'Tell me if it's none of my business, only I'm curious to know. Where are your ma and dad? And why do you think robbers are after you? Are you in trouble?'

Gwen could see no reason not to answer this kindly stranger's question. 'Our da is dead, drowned, and our ma is a long way from here,' she said. 'I'm Gwen, and this is my brother, Mark. We're trying to reach the Citadel of Ilatias because we need to talk to the Sleih king.'

The stallholder's grey eyebrows rose high, as if wanting to

join up with what remained of his short grey hair. All he said, however, was, 'My name's Melthrop Kaine, pie maker and travelling food purveyor, at your service.'

They all shook hands.

'I don't live here,' Melthrop said. 'I live nearer the Citadel, in a village called Darnel. Camped just outside here for now.' He stood back, plump hands on his broad hips. 'Why don't you stay with me tonight and tell me what's going on? Might be able to help.'

Gwen chewed her lip. It would be good to have help in this strange country. And somewhere other than the side of the road to sleep. She glanced at Mark.

He gave a short nod.

***

Gwen squashed between Mark and Melthrop Kaine as the heavy cart trundled out of the village to a field where other market visitors camped with their wagons and horses.

'This village is called Faren,' Melthrop Kaine said. 'Short for Far End because it's the last village before the forests when you travel south from the Citadel.'

Small fires ringed the camping field and men, women, children and dogs visited between them sharing the remnants of their market stalls and gossiping about how good or bad trading had been.

The scene put Gwen in mind of the robber camp, although far more cheerful and a lot cleaner.

Was it safer though?

Gwen squinted into the smoky twilight. Were the robbers here, somewhere, in this crowd? She ducked her head and spread her and Mark's cloaks in the deeper shadows under the cart.

After a picnic supper of cold meat, cheese and cake eaten at a low table, Gwen asked, 'How far is it to the Citadel of Ilatias from here?'

'The Citadel?' Melthrop Kaine leaned his elbow on his neat, black-trousered knee and stroked his plump chin. 'Why, it all depends on which way you go and how you go. If I was a Sleih lord on his fancy horse, it would take me no time at all. However, as I'm an old Madach with a heavy cart and a slow old horse, it's going to take me the best part of four days' easy travel. And if I stop at any market towns on the way, well, it could take days.'

'Good,' Gwen said. 'Not too much further to go.'

***

Melthrop handed his guests hot mugs of tea. 'Can I ask why you young ones are off to Ilatias to see the Sleih king?'

'It's for our people,' Gwen said. 'We hope the Sleih will help us.' She glanced at her brother who briefly closed his eyes and went on eating cake.

Melthrop believed an important decision had been taken. He waited, sipping at his tea.

Finally, Gwen said, 'I hope this will be all right, telling you ...' She paused, then, in a rush, 'Can I ask if you know of the Danae?'

Melthrop lowered his mug to the table.

'The Danae? The fairy folk?'

Gwen sighed. 'Yes, the Danae. And we're not fairy folk.'

'You're ....?' Melthrop wondered if he himself had strolled into a fairytale.

'We believed the Sleih were a fairytale,' Mark said. 'Now we know they're not, although we knew about the Madach and we supposed all Madach were evil because they threw the Danae out of The Place Before, which we think is the country around the Citadel, and we have to ask the Sleih for help.'

Gwen rolled her eyes and Melthrop Kaine scratched his stubbled head.

'I know the old tales of the Danae,' he said, 'and how they left the kingdom a long, long time ago. People think it's merely

111

an old story, or if something did happen it was so long ago nobody knows any more exactly what it was. Certainly, no one thinks there are any Danae left, if they existed at all.'

He studied the two of them. 'You're telling me you're Danae?'

It was true their summer-tanned faces and slim builds gave them a look of the Sleih. However, their brown and copper hair said otherwise. He'd assumed they were Madach, and it had troubled him, wondering where their parents were and why they were filthy and ragged. He'd been certain they must be lost. Now, they were telling him ...?

Melthrop laughed. 'Danae, at my campfire. Fancy!'

He became suddenly serious. 'You must not say this to anyone else. There are people who would love to get their hands on two young Danae, sell them to the highest bidder as fairytale slaves. Promise me?'

'We know,' Mark said.

'It's part of our story too,' Gwen said. 'Madach in the Deep Forest caught us and they were going to sell us, or at least me. The wolves saved us.'

'The wolves ...?' Once more Melthrop Kaine had that wandering into a fairytale, or perhaps a dream, feeling.

'Why don't you tell me from the beginning?' he said. 'It seems you've had a pretty rough time, and you're only kids after all, no offence meant' (as Mark had pulled a face at this) 'and all by yourselves. If you feel you can trust me, maybe I can help. What do you think?'

Gwen smiled. 'We would love your help, thank you.'

***

The camp had quietened by the time they finished their tale. Melthrop Kaine asked few questions, a cold mug of tea in his hand, nodding and shaking his head by turns.

'I'd planned on starting my way back home tomorrow,' he said. 'I'll take you to the Citadel, see you safely there.'

'Do you think the king will see us?' Mark said.

Melthrop tossed the dregs of his tea onto the grass, stood and hitched his trousers higher over his belly.

'Hard to say. The Sleih can be strange,' he said, echoing Josh's sentiment. 'Right now, though, it's time for sleep. The camp wakes early.'

Gwen was finding it hard to stay awake and Mark was yawning hugely. The warm summer night, the soft glow of the fire's coals and a full stomach had her agreeing with Melthrop Kaine that it was time for sleep. She crept right under the cart, encouraging Mark to do the same.

'In case those robbers are about.'

Chapter Twenty One

It All Goes Wrong

'Tell us about the Citadel,' Gwen said.

'Josh says the streets are paved with gold and the houses built of marble and precious stones, with windows made of diamonds,' Mark said. 'Is that true?'

The cart was heading north, the old horse plodding steadily forward. In the far distance the white tips of the mountains were becoming clearer.

Melthrop chuckled. 'Not quite, although it's a lovely place with its main road curving up to the King's Tower. There're tall stone houses all the way along, and although their windows aren't made of diamonds, they're certainly grand places.'

Gwen found it hard to imagine. The Madach farm houses were grand enough.

'Is the Citadel big?' she said. 'If Lucy's there, will we be able to find her?'

'Ah, could be tricky.' Melthrop paused, clicking on the reins to move the slow old horse along. 'We'll have to see when we get there.'

Gwen could feel his discomfort. She suspected Melthrop Kaine believed Lucy had been stolen away by Madach robbers.

About midday, Melthrop pulled the cart off the road opposite a small shop in a busy hamlet.

'Stay here,' he said, tying a full nose-bag around the horse's head. 'I'll do my business with the shopkeeper and then we'll fetch a bite of lunch.'

He dodged a laden cart and crossed the road.

Gwen watched him go, and gasped. 'Mark, those Madach who chased us yesterday, they're here, outside the shop! They've seen us.'

Mark swung around. 'Do you think we should shout, or run?'

Too late. The Madach, mounted on big brown horses, were at the cart. And they were doing their own shouting, although not much of it made sense.

'There you are! At last! Young scoundrels! Your mother is frantic, worried to death about the two of you! The master has a mind to whip you both, fretting your mother like this! Come on, out of there and home with us!'

One seized Mark. The other tugged at Gwen's arm.

Gwen tugged back. 'Get off! Leave us alone!'

Mark kicked out wildly.

People stopped to watch. An old man hurried up, demanding to know what was happening.

The Madach with greying blonde hair brandished a riding crop at him.

'Don't worry, sir. These naughty children think it's funny to worry their poor parents by running away, pretending to be beggars.'

He wielded the crop near Mark's head. 'Wherever did you find these rags?'

His horse pranced about, and Gwen, wrestling with the Madach trying to haul her onto his horse, saw it was too dangerous for the old man to come closer.

'He's lying,' she shouted. 'Get our friend, in with the shopkeeper, he knows us. Please!'

The old man looked to the shop, and quickly back to where the grey-haired Madach had swung Mark over his saddle and was trotting down the road.

The crowd scattered, protesting.

Gwen couldn't leave Mark, not a second time. She let herself be lifted out of the cart.

Something went 'ping'.

Gwen wondered briefly, while yelling at the old man, 'Please! Get our friend!'

The robber cantered down the road.

The last face Gwen saw, before her head was forced into the horse's sweaty neck, belonged to Melthrop Kaine. He stood in the road, staring after them, mouth open in horror.

***

'Shut up and you won't get hurt,' the robber said. 'And your brother won't either.'

Gwen shut up.

They galloped back down the road, heading south. Gwen knew people must be staring and once or twice she heard someone shout, objecting at being nearly ridden over. The riders ignored them, occasionally calling, 'On his master's business, make way there.'

After some time, Gwen sensed the horse turn off the main road. They rode for a while longer before the rider stopped, jumped down and pulled Gwen after him in one quick movement. He pushed her arms behind her back. She cried out, forced to bend over with the pain.

Mark was there, also on his feet, and trying to kick the robber holding him. The robber chuckled and held Mark at arm's length.

'Good work, hey, Chester?' The robber grinned. 'Ours now, do what we want with 'em.'

'What's going on?' Gwen tried to sound haughty. It was hard while she was squirming in the robber's grasp. 'What do you want with us? We haven't anything of value. Let us go.'

She wasn't surprised when Chester said, 'Think I'd forgotten you, hey? Not at all, not at all.' He shook Mark, roughly. 'And it seems this one didn't drown after all. Good news for us. Two Danae, exactly what we need.'

He beamed. 'The same little Danae who got the best of our friends before. Terribly embarrassed they were, losing you'–he winked at Gwen, full of good humour–'and with stories of wolves chasing 'em while never a scratch on either of 'em.'

Chester's friend leered at Gwen. 'How did you escape?'

Gwen straightened up, trying to appear unafraid. 'The wolves rescued us, both of us.'

Chester guffawed. 'Sense of humour, like it! Could sell you to a king as a joker, if I didn't have other plans for you.'

Other plans like selling them to the woman who wanted them. Who was she? Why did she want them?

Chester stopped laughing. 'Right, this is what's gonna happen. We're gonna let you ride up front of us, comfortable like, with your hands tied. Any nonsense and it'll be bags over the heads and across the saddle, like before.'

Gwen and Mark were hauled back onto the horses, their hands tied and covered with rugs to hide the bindings. They passed few people. Each time they did, Chester said, 'Show your manners, children and offer these folk a courtesy,' at which Gwen and Mark were forced to say, 'Good day,' and nod politely.

One farmer's wife on a fat white mare and with baskets before and after her, was more curious than the other travellers. She stopped, forcing the robbers to stop too. Her generous lips pursed at the sight of the two dirty young people.

'Well, goodness me, whatever have these children been up to?'

'Master Denton's two rascals, madam.' Chester smiled. 'Run off from their nanny, for a joke, causing Mistress Denton untold grief. Caught up with them finally and taking them back home to their lady mother and worthy father, who'll give them a good telling off and put them to bed with no supper,

I dare say.'

'Well, I never.' The farmer's wife wagged a finger at Mark. 'You mind yourself, and don't give your poor mother any more grief, do you hear?'

Mark glared.

'Help us!' Gwen started to cry out. All that came from her mouth was a pained squeak. The robber had pinched her fiercely.

The farmer's wife passed by, shaking her head. The kidnappers cantered on. Gwen and Mark bounced uncomfortably on the horses' wide backs.

They moved swiftly past two farm houses and a handful of small cottages. A short way further on, the track began to weave between young, thinly spaced trees. Their way became no more than a narrow trail with barely room for the horses to go in single file. The trees became bigger. There were more of them.

Gwen's heart was heavy. They were heading back into the forest. And there were no friendly foxes to guide them out should they manage to escape these determined robbers.

Chapter Twenty Two

Melthrop Kaine's Unhappiness

It was Melthrop Kaine's turn to shout.

'What were you all doing, letting those children be kidnapped in broad daylight?'

Many in the crowd found the ground interesting. Others had to urgently hurry back to their tasks.

The old man who had tried to help said, 'I knew it wasn't right, but they spun this story and the horses were prancing around. Couldn't get near the kids.'

Melthrop sighed. 'Thanks for trying.' He gazed around for inspiration. 'What to do, what to do?'

Something winked up at him from the dusty ground. He bent to retrieve it and found himself holding a thin silver chain with a delicate pendant hanging from it. A memory came to him, from yesterday, of seeing the chain around Gwen's neck when she was cutting the cake for supper. At the time, he'd been surprised this dirty, tattered girl wore a silver chain. Afterwards, he'd forgotten about it in listening to their story.

Melthrop held the pendant up to see it better. A gryphon, with a silver body, exquisite blue sapphire feathers and tiny green emerald eyes. A pretty piece which would fetch a high price in any fancy jewellery shop in the Citadel. He wondered how a young girl from the edge of nowhere came by such an ornament. He tucked it into his shirt pocket for safe-keeping.

He'd make sure she got it back. Yes, he would.

The crowd had dispersed, including the old man. The horse had munched its way through the nose bag and was waiting for a drink. Melthrop Kaine led the horse and the cart to the water trough and stood patiently, thinking.

He knew he couldn't abandon two children. He was the one friend Gwen and Mark had here.

When the horse had finished, Melthrop climbed up onto his seat and headed back the way he'd come. He pushed the cart as fast as the old horse and the heavy traffic allowed, asking everyone he came across if they'd seen two riders bearing two dirty, unkempt children.

He'd gone some way when he came across a farmer's wife on a fat white mare and with baskets before and after her. He hailed her. 'Have you seen a couple of rough-looking men with two children travelling this way?'

The farmer's wife pulled up her mare.

'Oh, those naughty kiddies. What did they do? Steal your pies?'

'Pardon?' Melthrop said. 'Have you seen them? What did the men say?'

'Why,' the farmer's wife said, 'they told me the children were Master and Mistress Denton's rascals – though come to think of it, I don't know any Dentons around here – and they'd run off for a joke and their poor mother was out of her mind with worry. They were taking them home, and the brats didn't seem at all grateful.'

'Thank you. Was that a while back?'

'Oh yes. I was on the track from home, heading to the road.'

'Heading to the road? Where, madam, please, it's extremely important? Those poor children haven't run away from home at all. They've been kidnapped.'

The farmer's wife clasped her plump hand to her bosom. 'Truly?' Her attitude to the brats somersaulted. 'Oh, poor things! They must have been terrified when I saw them. No wonder they didn't say anything, afraid for their lives no doubt.'

'Where did you see them, please, madam?'

'Keep on, for a good couple of miles at least, and there's an old oak by a stile and a track leading off. They were going along there when I met them.'

'And where does that lead, please?'

'Our farm, our neighbour's farm, and then it goes off into the forest, where it doesn't go anywhere much. A few labourers' cottages and trees. It'll be hard to find them in there.' She frowned.

'I'd best be on my way as quick as I can. Thank you for your help.' Melthrop waved at the farmer's wife and flicked the reins of the cart.

'Good luck,' she said. 'I do hope you find them, poor babes!' And she gee'd up her fat white mare to ride leisurely northwards, shaking her head.

Melthrop Kaine hurried on, his way made slow by the crowded road. He soon realised he'd never noticed before how many stiles were to be found by oaks. It was a long time until he finally came to one which had a track leading off.

At last.

He cast an anxious glance at the sky where the sun had definitely passed its zenith.

'Plenty of time, won't be dark for ages,' he said to the horse, which was making good use of this opportunity by cropping the grass beneath the oak.

Melthrop didn't give the horse long. He drove as fast as he could, past the neat farms, past the labourers' cottages, right to the edge of the forest. There he stopped, got down and peered along the narrowing trail.

'Won't be getting you down there.' He patted the horse's neck as it nibbled this new grass. 'Not with the cart anyway.'

Melthrop looked long at the horse. 'Ride you?' The horse lifted its head from the grass, blinked and went on cropping.

Melthrop sighed. He had no saddle and the horse wasn't used to being ridden. He either had to walk, or go back.

He took water and a bucket from the back of the cart and watched the horse drink thirstily. His hand on the horse's neck, he pondered what to do. His chances of finding Gwen and Mark in the vast expanse of trees were slim, especially if he had to walk.

And if he found them, how was he going to rescue them from the robbers? He didn't have enough money to buy them.

Likely, he would be taken captive himself and sold alongside the Danae.

The horse, finished drinking, stamped its feet and nuzzled Melthrop's back.

'Time to go?' Melthrop said.

He put the bucket in the back and climbed into the cart. He sat there, arguing with himself. No, he decided, it wouldn't help Gwen and Mark if he went blundering into the forest in search of a needle in a haystack. He had to find another way to help. Although what?

With a great deal of reluctance and a strong sense of guilt, Melthrop turned the cart around and made his way back to the main road. Here he headed north, troubled by anxious thoughts about the fate of his new friends.

They might escape, he hoped, and make their way to the Citadel. He'd comb the Citadel for them and if they weren't there, he'd take himself off on an adventure, go to the slave countries and search for them. It would be his life mission!

Melthrop grew excited at the prospect – until night fell and with it a deep sense of loss and helplessness. He jumped heavily down, lit lamps at the back and front of the cart, hoisted himself back into his seat, and gee'd the horse up once more.

Chapter Twenty Three

Isa Wants A Friend

The summer sun was still well above the horizon when the Madach horsemen cantered into their camp with their weary captives.

Isa ran up, tangled red hair flying.

'You found her! And the other one as well! Not drowned? Da'll be pleased!'

Chester growled at her. 'Your da ain't got nothing to do with it this time, missy Isa. These Danae are ours, captured fair, and ours to do what we want with 'em.'

Isa pouted. 'P'rhaps. Except who found them in the first place? My da. Anyway, who cares about two puny Danae when Da and Uncle Viv are finding lots and lots more down by the sea.'

They went, after all, Mark thought. He wasn't worried about two Madach robbers stealing the Danae. Tomas would soon send them off, supposing the robbers actually found the villages. What did worry him was whether anyone was left to steal.

Chester interrupted Mark's worrying. He jumped down from the horse and pulled Mark after him. The other robber pushed Gwen off his horse. She landed in a heap at Isa's feet.

Mark reached for her. 'Gwen!'

Chester squeezed Mark's shoulder, holding him back.

'Take the girl to a tent,' he said to Isa, 'and find her something to eat. And tie her up, because if she escapes, it'll be on your head.'

Isa lunged for the rope around Gwen's hands and stomped off with her to the other side of the camp, beaming.

Mark watched Gwen go, his stomach hollow.

'You can go in the cage.' Chester smirked and beckoned to a stout boy nearby. 'You, Alec, take this one to the cage and make sure the door's bolted tight. You're his guard, got it?'

Alec, puffed up with pride, hauled Mark to a sturdy cage of willow branches at the edge of the camp, checked his hands were tied tight and thrust him inside.

Mark slumped to the dirt floor.

What would happen to him and Gwen now? Sold, fairytale slaves?

The hollow feeling in his stomach deepened.

***

Gwen yanked at her bindings to twist around and see what was happening. A stout boy was pulling Mark to the edge of the forest and Chester was calling to a young man coming out of a tent.

'Hey you, Jack,' Chester said. 'Got a job for you. Take the fastest horse. Message to be sent, urgent.'

Isa hustled Gwen into the hot and stuffy tent, pushed her across the dirt floor and tied her arms to a thick pole going through the roof. She stepped back and eyed her captive.

'The others poked fun at my da and Uncle Viv because of you,' she said.

Gwen wanted to say, 'Good.' She bit the retort back. She didn't want to end up in a cage too.

Isa circled the pole. She reached out a dirty hand and stroked Gwen's hair. Gwen tossed her head and Isa drew back her hand as if Gwen had bitten her.

'Well, I guess Chester's gonna sell you to the Blue Lady,' Isa said, 'which is a shame 'cos I could've taken care of you, like I told Da before. But no, he wanted to sell you and you escaped and now Chester's found you and I won't ever get the chance to look after you.' She gave a great sigh. Her hand moved once more to Gwen's hair.

Gwen steeled herself not to jerk her head away. A plan of sorts was shaping among the desolate thoughts going round and round in her head.

When Gwen submitted to being patted, Isa grinned, showing uneven and dirty teeth.

'Before Chester takes you away,' she said, 'we can have a chat and you can tell me what it's like being a fairytale.'

Gwen briefly closed her eyes, steeling herself to be nice.

'Well?' Isa prodded. 'Got nothing to say?'

Gwen's plan firmed up. She gave a sad, small smile. 'I'm sorry, Isa.'

Isa's eyes lit up at this use of her name.

'Me and my brother,' Gwen said, 'have had a really bad time and we don't know what this Chester plans on doing with us, and Mark's out there in a cage like an animal. It makes it hard to be friendly and talk.'

Isa nodded, her red curls bobbing up and down. 'Yeah, I see.'

Gwen bowed her head. 'Who's the Blue Lady? Why does she want us?'

'Don't remember her name.' Isa scowled. 'She came here looking for Danae children, is all I know.' She leaned close to Gwen. 'She was horribly scary.'

'Isa!' a woman called from outside. 'What you doing in there? Come and help with the food. Now!'

Isa's scowl directed itself at the tent opening. 'Don't go anywhere.' She giggled and pushed her way outside.

Gwen closed her eyes and let them stay closed. What would happen to her and Mark?

Her arms ached. She was hungry and thirsty.

125

And furious.

How did they end up back with the robbers? Right when it was all going well ... with someone to help them ... so close, and now ... Gwen stamped her foot. Why hadn't they been more careful?

She wriggled to see if she could loosen the rope. It gripped tighter. How could she escape? What was happening to Mark? Was their new friend Melthrop Kaine doing something to find them? Although what could he do ...?

Isa re-appeared with two bowls of hot stew. She put the bowls on the floor and came close to Gwen.

'I'm gonna untie you so's you can sit down and eat, but I'm gonna tie your legs in case you've been thinking of escaping before we've had our chat.'

Gwen wearily nodded her understanding. When she was sitting on the floor with her ankles tied, Isa handed her a bowl. Gwen had eaten nothing since breakfast. She took the bowl and followed Isa's lead by slurping at it from the rim. It tasted slightly better than it smelled.

'Will my brother get something to eat?'

Isa shrugged. 'Probably. Depends on whether Alec remembers.' She paused from her slurping. 'He usually does. Don't worry.'

Gwen tried another small, sad smile. 'Good,' she said. She worried about the 'usually'. Did they have lots of captives in cages?

Lucy!

'Can I ask you a question?'

Isa's eyes narrowed. 'Depends. Chester says I shouldn't tell you anything.'

'Have you ever had a young woman here with golden curls and blue eyes? From the Forest?'

'No. Is she a Danae too?'

'No, no. She's someone we met on our journey.'

'Hmm.'

There was a moment's silence before Isa said, 'Why are you on a journey, anyway? Where're you and your brother going?'

Gwen hesitated. Her hazy plan didn't include telling Isa anything much at all.

'Well?' Isa said. 'You must have a reason for being far from home.'

'Yes, we do.'

Tears welled. Real ones. What was happening at home? Was everyone safe? Still there?

'Our families are in trouble,' Gwen said, 'and we need to find help. Invaders have come to our Forest and we believe they'll drive us from our homes.'

'Oh.' Isa frowned, then grinned. 'P'rhaps you should be like us and not have a proper home. We can go wherever we like. Can't be driven out, neither.'

The vision which popped into Gwen's head of her mother in a dirty tent cooking over an open fire in all weathers, almost turned her tears to smiles.

'We're not like you,' she said. 'Our families grow things and keep livestock and we have a mill for making flour for bread and a forge for making all kinds of things. We couldn't move those around.'

'But you're a fairytale. Don't you have magic to help you?'

'We're not fairytales. We're normal people living normal lives.'

'You don't live in palaces? No magic?'

'No magic,' Gwen said. Callie, and Verian, came to her mind and she wondered if it was true there was no magic in the Danae.

'Who's in your family besides your brother?' Isa said.

'Ma, and our two sisters.'

'No da?'

'Our da drowned, at sea.'

Isa bit her lip. 'You don't have a da and I don't have a ma.' She patted Gwen's hand. 'We're the same, you and me.' She heaved a great sigh. 'It's a real shame about the Blue Lady.'

Chapter Twenty Four

A Badger, An Owl And Dogs

Mark couldn't stretch his legs. After two nights and days the ache was unbearable. He was hungry, thirsty, and damp from the day's rain. The boy guarding him had finally thrown an old blanket over the top of the willow cage. The blanket had stopped the sun, when it made an appearance late in the afternoon, from drying Mark out.

He shut his eyes on the sight of the robber camp and strained to hear the one noise among the forest noises he most wanted to hear.

No howls of wolves, close by or distant, came to him.

Only a breathy snuffling.

A black-eyed badger stared at Mark from the edge of the trees. Mark stared back.

'Badger, can you understand me, like you can Josh?'

The badger blinked.

Encouraged, Mark went on. 'We need help here, if you can.'

The badger stared.

Mark sighed. What could a badger do?

***

The badger waved its long snout from side to side and shambled back into the trees. Its sluggish brain worked hard to remember a story about a couple of foxes looking after two children who had to get to the place called the Citadel. The badger didn't know who the children were, or why they had to be looked after. In the badger's experience, two-legged children could take care of themselves. It did know it was important to other animals for these children to reach the Citadel. The badger also knew this wasn't going to happen if they were in a Madach cage. It knew too well what happened if you ended up in a Madach cage.

The badger snuffled at the ground. Yes, it supposed it had better do something. Now it scampered through the forest night, searching for what it knew would be there, in the dark.

Not long after, an owl flew down to a farmyard and perched on the eaves of the house.

'Hoo, whoo, are you there?' the owl hooted at the sleeping farm dogs.

The dogs woke, barking.

The farmhouse door opened.

'What is it, boys and girls? Is it a fox?'

The dogs had already stopped barking. Just an owl.

The farmer went inside. The dogs settled back to sleep.

The owl hooted again. 'Listen, listen. The children, the ones we're supposed to be minding. The robber Madach have them. They're in danger. You have to help.'

The dogs came fully awake. They understood. It seemed all the animals, wild and farm, knew of these children. Those foxes had talked all the time, even when they were raiding Madach farms for chickens and running from the dogs.

Quietly, to avoid disturbing the farmer and his wife, the farm dogs climbed over the fence or scrambled under the gate and sprinted up the track to the forest, tails high.

The owl went back to its hunting.

By the time the dogs arrived at the Madach camp all was quiet. Everyone, including Mark in his cage and Gwen in the tent with Isa, was asleep.

The robbers' dogs sniffed the new scents and did not move

from their places outside their masters' tents.

The farm dogs settled by the fire to wait.

***

Lady Melda bestowed a condescending smirk on the young Madach boy standing in her hall. She liked the way he twisted his hands together and kept his head down. She liked better the message he brought.

Eyes on the shining marble floor, the boy mumbled, 'Chester says to tell you, m'lady, we got the two Danae children you want. He says to come to our camp, to collect them, like you said you would.'

Lady Melda's heart pounded. She had them!

'Certainly, I will come immediately,' she said to the boy, whose notions of rewards of gold and silver radiated from him in a brilliant glow. She smiled. 'Tell your Chester there will be rewards enough for all, once I have the two Danae in my charge.'

The boy blushed, bowed clumsily, and tumbled down the wide steps in his rush to leave the house.

Lady Melda summoned a servant. 'Prepare my horse,' she said. 'I will be gone a day or two.'

***

As the sun sent out its first pink rays of the new day, a woman crawled from her tent in the Madach robber camp and headed to the fire.

She heard the unfamiliar dogs before she saw them.

They growled, fiercely, from deep in their chests. They bared their teeth and their hackles rose.

'Help!' The woman backed off in a great hurry.

People stumbled, bleary-eyed, from tents all over the camp. They shouted, waved their arms and called for their own dogs to deal with the invading vicious dogs.

Their own dogs were nowhere to be seen.

Gwen, inside the tent with Isa, assumed it was the robbers' dogs making all the noise.

Was someone trying to rob the robbers?

She glanced at Isa. The Madach girl was fast asleep. One arm trailed over the side of her low bed.

The arm was tied to Gwen's leg, barely. During the night Gwen had stubbornly picked at the knot, stopping whenever Isa murmured in her sleep.

Gwen frowned at the tent flap, and back at the knot.

Whatever was going on, it might be her one chance to escape.

Although if it went wrong, her efforts at pretending to be friends with Isa in the hope the girl would help them, would be worse than wasted.

Too bad.

Gwen plucked at the last bits of rope. The final strand came free.

Isa woke up.

'What?' she mumbled, tugging at the rope.

'What?' she said again, louder, scrambling from the bed.

She lunged for Gwen.

'No you don't!'

Gwen wrenched around to look straight into Isa's wild eyes.

The yelling and barking outside was a solid cacophony of noise.

Isa let go of Gwen and ran to the opening. Gwen ran after her.

Isa pushed her aside, a finger to her mouth. 'Let me see what's goin' on.'

Gwen hung back, ready to leap forward.

Isa pulled the flap open the merest crack, put her eye to the opening, gasped and shut the flap.

'Wild dogs, attacking the camp,' she said. 'Best stay here, safer.'

'No!' Gwen tried to push past Isa. 'Let me go, Isa, let me go.'

Isa grabbed Gwen's arms. 'Let you go?' She shook her sleep-tangled curls. 'An' why would I let you go? Chester'd tie me to a stake and beat me black and blue if I let you go.'

Gwen held Isa's gaze. 'You said yourself, we're the same. Would you let this Blue Lady take you? Wouldn't you fight, to save your family?'

Isa narrowed her eyes.

'Whatever the cost?' Gwen said, softly.

'Truly, you think we're the same?' Isa's hold on Gwen's arms loosened.

Outside the tent the frenzy of barking and shouting rose higher.

'Yes.' Gwen nodded hard. 'Help me, Isa.'

Isa's scowl softened. 'The same?' She sniffed, and lifted her grubby chin high. 'Okay, I'll do it. I don't care about old Chester.' She dropped her hands from Gwen's arms.

Gwen managed to smile back. Her whole body yearned to bolt through that tent opening.

Isa tugged at the flap.

Gwen darted forward, but Isa grabbed her shoulder. Gwen's heart plummeted.

'And if Chester catches you,' Isa said, apparently caring about old Chester after all, 'you kicked me real hard and escaped, right?'

'Yes, yes, of course.'

Gwen struggled free and burst through. She glanced at the wild dogs and the terrified Madach, and ran, around the edge of the camp to where she prayed she'd find Mark.

In the middle of the camp, the dogs howled and snarled. The Madach lashed out with sticks and stones and yells.

Gwen kept running. She prayed the dogs wouldn't attack her.

She reached the cage. Mark was kicking at the bars.

'Hurry, hurry! The dogs are helping us. Hurry!'

Gwen slid the bolt, pulled her brother out and helped him stand. He swayed, awkward with his bound hands and stiff legs.

The dogs bayed at the robbers.

On the other side of the camp, Gwen glimpsed Isa already limping from her tent, waving and calling. No one took any notice. The robbers' attention was all on the dogs.

One dog detached itself from the pack and ran at Gwen and Mark.

Gwen's already thudding heart beat faster. 'Watch out!'

Mark grinned. 'It's all right!'

Relief, and puzzlement, swept through Gwen when the dog ran past them, into the forest. At the edge of the trees, it whirled about and barked like a mad thing.

'Let's go!' Mark staggered after the dog.

Gwen at last took in what Mark had been shouting. The dogs were helping them!

'Hey, over there!' Chester's scream carried above the barking of the dogs and the yelling of the robbers. 'They're running away! Our prisoners are escaping!'

Gwen ran, chasing the dog and Mark out of the camp into the trees. Nettles stung her arms and legs. Mark stumbled and Gwen hauled him up, urging him along.

They ran and ran, hard on the dog's flying tail, racing through stands of young trees where thin branches whipped Gwen's face, across rivulets of water where she slipped on wet stones and mud, and on to a narrow trail.

Behind them, the baying and screaming grew slowly, too slowly, fainter.

Chapter Twenty Five

Dorothy And Dan

A stitch in Gwen's side racked every step with pain. Her breath came in rasping grunts. At last she and Mark fell out onto the track by the small cottages.

The dog flopped onto its belly, panting, tongue lolling, black lips curled in a grin.

Gwen arched her body, pressing her hand to her side and watching more dogs weave through the trees to collapse in a heap at her feet.

She scanned the track and the trees.

No robber Madach on horses came thundering through. The only sounds were her and Mark's heavy breathing and the dogs' panting.

The dogs bounced up, tails wagging. They thrust wet noses into Gwen's hands and jumped up at Mark, whose bindings caused him to topple over. He plumped heavily onto the dirt, laughing.

'Thank you, thank you,' Gwen cried, over and over.

Mark waved his tied hands and chattered about badgers and how clever they were. The dogs weren't interested and neither was Gwen. She hugged and patted their rescuers. The dogs licked her face in return.

Two of the dogs sprinted further up the track. The others nudged Gwen and pushed at Mark to make him stand.

Gwen helped Mark up. She gently touched his hands, red

135

and swollen above the tight bindings.

'Your poor hands,' she said, hurrying after the dogs. 'The first thing is to get you untied.'

'Listen,' Mark said. 'Someone's calling the dogs.'

***

The calls came from behind a closed farm gate.

'Sammy, Harley, Phoebe, Daisy, where are you? Come here, come here, where are you?'

The dogs jumped over the gate or wriggled under it. They bounded between the gate and the farmhouse door, back and forth, leaping and barking, dancing around the farmer as if to say, See what we found! Aren't we clever?

The farmer gazed at the two filthy, tattered young people standing by his gate. He called over his shoulder to someone in the house. The farmer's wife came to the door.

'Well, by the Beings!' She waved a tea towel. 'If it isn't the two lost children from market day. Do you remember, Father, I told you about them? I told you how those wicked robbers kidnapped these poor kiddies and the nice man was searching for them and the wicked robbers told me a story about how they'd run away and their mother was distraught, and it seems they didn't, run away I mean, or have a mother, at least not one who was distraught, and in any case they shouldn't have been kidnapped.'

Talking all the time, the farmer's wife made her way across the yard, unlocked the gate and let Mark and Gwen in. Gwen remembered meeting her on the road and how she'd told them off for worrying their poor mother. It appeared she'd since met Melthrop Kaine and learned the truth.

The farmer's wife shoo'd them into a cluttered kitchen which smelled of baking bread and ushered them into seats at a table spread with a huge fresh loaf, pats of butter, bowls of jams and a pot of tea under a colourful tea cosy.

She tut-tutted at the sight of Mark's hands. Scissors were

136

produced together with a bowl of warm, aromatic water. The farmer's wife set about cutting through the rope and bathing and bandaging Mark's hands, muttering about wicked robbers and what a frightening experience they must have had, and how did they escape and how hungry they must be, did those horrible robbers feed them at all?

Gwen and Mark nodded and shook their heads and said, 'Mmm,' from time to time.

Finally the farmer's wife said to Gwen. 'Come along, your hands aren't in any shape to touch food either.' She used two fingers to hold one offending hand by the wrist.

The farmer came in from giving the dogs their breakfast. He eyed his unexpected and filthy visitors curiously.

'Well well well,' he said. 'You look like a couple of robber brats yourselves, if I'm honest. But if my dogs reckon you're worth rescuing, I guess I'll be glad to help you young 'uns if I can.'

And he started in on his own breakfast while his wife led Gwen into the scullery to get cleaned up and Mark clumsily and enthusiastically tucked into the fresh bread and butter.

***

Isa and the young boy who was supposed to guard Mark, stood with heads down, feet shuffling in the dirt. A livid Chester loomed over them.

'It was the dogs, Chester!' Isa said. 'What were we s'posed to do against wild dogs?'

'First wolves, now dogs. Anybody'd think those dirty little Danae are animals, not ... not ...' Chester searched for the word '... people.'

'P'rhaps they're not people,' the boy said, daring to glance up at Chester. Chester's glare made him lower his head.

Isa bravely took up the idea. 'They're s'posed to be fairytales, right? P'rhaps they can't be caught.'

'Of course! No doubt absolutely right, young Isa. Tell me

though'—all the camp heard him—'what we're gonna say to this lady from the Citadel when Jack brings her back, hey? What? We gonna tell her wild dogs came and freed her two Danae?'

He bent closer to Isa and the boy. 'You think she'll say, all calm like, Oh well, never mind, poor Chester, we'll be patient and wait for another chance to catch 'em?'

Chester raised his hand.

Isa flinched, took a step back. 'Can't we try and hunt 'em down? They can't be far.'

The boy nodded hard. 'I'll go, I'll find 'em Chester, I will.'

Chester, his hand high, snorted. 'Really? Really? Where you gonna look, hey? In all of this.' The hand moved in a circle, embracing the forest all around them. 'An' if they're not lost in there, they're gonna be with those dogs, aren't they?' He cuffed the boy across the arm and stamped back to the fire.

Yes, they could try and re-capture their prisoners before the lady arrived. What chance though? Maybe, Chester hoped fervently, the lady would be happy to wait and see what Viv and his brother brought back from their journey to the home of the Danae. Maybe the promise of more Danae, not merely these two scrawny children, would placate her.

He hoped.

***

After breakfast, the farmer's wife Dorothy set Gwen and Mark to feeding the chickens and hunting for eggs.

The simple chore reminded Gwen strongly of home.

What was happening there? she worried, scattering grain among the clucking birds. Was Callie feeding the chickens and helping their mother? Gwen stopped throwing grain and gazed to the east, where the sun was still climbing into the vivid blue sky. Were the Danae still in the Forest? Or had they been dragged away, bound and cowed, like in Callie's dreams ... she thrust her dismal imaginings aside to think instead about their early morning rescue by the dogs.

'Mark?' Gwen plunged a hand into the sack of grain. 'Why did the dogs rescue us? And how did they find us?'

'The badger, like I've been trying to tell you. I saw a badger watching me and I told it to fetch help. Like Josh would have done.'

'A badger? Did you know what it was thinking?'

'No, of course not. I just know it worked.'

The forest creatures might help you, Callie had said the night Gwen and Mark escaped the village. A boar had saved them from the bear and eagles had saved them from the chasm. Then there were the foxes on the bridge, the fox which had winked at Gwen. Now badgers and dogs?

Did the pendant help? Gwen wondered. It was meant to protect the wearer.

She reached for the necklace.

What?

She felt all the way around her neck.

'No!'

Mark jumped at Gwen's cry. 'What, where? What's wrong?'

'My pendant, it's gone.' Gwen searched around her neck.

Nothing. Worse than nothing.

The tiny gryphon's loss hurt her like a tragedy. Almost as painful as when she believed Mark had drowned. Almost as painful as losing Da, or Lucy vanishing into the Forest.

Gwen stood among the pecking chickens, lips tight together. How would she ever face Josh?

***

At mid-morning Gwen and Mark, the farmer, Dan, and Dorothy gathered around the kitchen table with mugs of tea.

'You must tell us everything.' Dorothy pushed a plate of cakes at Mark, her eyes on Gwen.

Gwen had thought a lot about what they should tell these kind people. Mark wanted to tell everything, certain the farmer and his wife would do them no harm. After all, it had been their dogs which had rescued them. In the end Gwen agreed and told their whole adventure, although it had to be broken up into different tales because there were jobs to be done and Farmer Dan and Dorothy couldn't spend all day listening to stories.

'Danae?' the farmer said.

'Like in the fairytales?' Dorothy reached out a hand to touch Gwen's arm, as if to check she was flesh and blood.

It was late, well after supper, when finally all was told. Farmer Dan stretched out in his comfortable old chair near the unlit fire, sucking on an empty pipe.

Dorothy was silent, for a time. Then she shifted in her chair and said, briskly, 'Well, you must stay here for a day or two, at least to get you cleaned up.'

She'd already heated hot baths and taken their tattered clothes to wash and mend. She'd given them old shirts of Farmer Dan's to wear in the meantime.

'Dan,' Dorothy said, 'I'm sure the least we can do is take these young people along the road a ways to the Citadel, don't you think?'

'Certainly,' he said. 'Normally I'd take you all the way. Just can't leave the farm at this time of year.'

'Anything would help us.' Gwen was moved by their generous spirits. 'Especially if it takes us further from those robbers.'

'And whoever else wants us,' Mark said.

Chapter Twenty Six

The Blue Lady's Wrath

The camp's inhabitants froze into statues when the lady emerged from the woods on her tall, black horse. The dogs too, were motionless, ears back, on their bellies in the dirt.

Chester stepped out of his tent, casting around for the cause of the sudden hush. He saw the lady, lifted his head high, crossed his arms, and looked directly at her.

Isa sucked in her breath.

The lady avidly returned Chester's gaze. 'Where are they, my Danae, where do you have them?'

There was a long silence, during which Chester's arms fell limply to his sides. His head went down to his chest.

The lady dropped from her horse and strode up to Chester. 'Wild dogs? What do you mean, wild dogs?'

She reached out a slim finger to lift his head from his chest. Her sea-green eyes bore into his brown ones.

'Stupid!' She let Chester's head drop once more.

She wheeled around. And found Isa.

'You, girl, show me where these Danae were kept before these ... these *wild dogs*, freed them.'

Isa scuttled to the willow cage, its door hanging open.

The lady caressed the bars, tugged at the bolt, closed her eyes.

She swept her arm wide, opened her eyes, and stared at Isa. 'This was the boy. Where was the girl?'

Isa's face went white beneath her grimy freckles. She tramped sluggishly to her own tent, the one she shared with Da. The Blue Lady walked up beside her, closed her mouth tightly and pulled aside the dirty flap. She quickly withdrew her head, breathed out, and in the same instant shifted around to face Isa.

Isa was as tall as the lady, and much more solid. Nevertheless, it was Isa who crouched in the dirt, sobbing. 'Sorry, sorry, sorry.'

'Bah!' The lady drew back a foot as if she would kick Isa, apparently changed her mind, pivoted on her heel and walked back to her horse.

Chester had managed to raise his head, although it was doubtful he saw anything. Isa squirmed on her stomach in the dirt, crying, tearing at her hair. Everyone else was frozen, eyes wide, mouths open. The dogs didn't move an ear between them.

'Today you are fortunate,' the lady said. Her voice was hard as rock. 'Today, I will not destroy you. Only this.' She inclined her head towards Isa's tent.

The tent exploded in a flash of blue and silver.

The robbers came to life, screaming.

The lady cantered out of the camp, a spray of dust behind her.

142

Chapter Twenty Seven

Disappointments

'Do you think we'll get there today?' Mark said.

The air was hot, the dry road heavy with dust from all the wagons and horses and mules. Mark was glad to rest on a grassy bank when the sun was at its highest.

Farmer Dan had taken Mark and Gwen in his wagon as far as the next market town, where Dorothy had bid them an anxious goodbye and a fearful good luck with a fluttering of her colourful handkerchief and a bag each stuffed with bread, cheese, pasties and fruit.

The first two nights they'd slept in barns. On the third day, a merchant gave them a ride to the next village, where they scrambled into the loft of an abandoned stable to shelter for the night.

Gwen gazed northwards to where the high mountains rose on the far horizon, white-tipped and deeply blue against the vivid azure of the sky. She sipped from her water bottle and shrugged. 'It doesn't feel real we could be this close. Finally.'

The scent of success drove them fast despite the heat, as if the Citadel of Ilatias was a giant magnet pulling them along.

'Look,' Gwen said.

Mark lifted his head and realised he'd reached the crest of the steep hill which had taken forever to climb. Many travellers had halted after the strenuous ascent and people were sitting on the grassy verge pulling out waterskins and bottles.

Mark stared ahead. Below them stretched the familiar green plain criss-crossed with roads and tracks, hedges and farms and one or two villages. And in the distance he caught his first glimpse of the Citadel of Ilatias. The home of the Sleih.

Sand-coloured walls rose up from the green fields, terrace upon terrace of them forming their own mountain. High towers glinted in the bright afternoon sun, making Mark believe Josh's story about diamond windows. Beyond Ilatias, the white-capped alps enfolded the city in vast, protective arms. Mark was fascinated by their jagged peaks, stark against the deep blue of the summer sky.

He grinned. 'Come on, we're nearly there.'

Gwen was already hurrying down the hill. Mark ran to catch her up and they walked steadily on, side by side. The sand-coloured walls grew taller.

Mark's grin never faltered. They'd made it!

Crowds of Madach on carts, horses and on foot, jostled each other as they passed through a wide, arched gateway. Mark ran ahead of Gwen, eager to see what lay beyond the walls. Once inside, he stopped, right in the road, taking in the sights and sounds and smells.

'Out of the way there, boy!' A scowling black-haired rider pulled on jewel-studded reins to swerve around Mark.

Mark scrambled to the side of the road. He stared after the horse and rider.

Gwen joined him there. 'Those people, the ones with the black hair.' She waved at a group of slim men and women with skin the colour of golden honey. They were dressed in brightly coloured clothes which floated around them like gossamer wings. Their arms and necks were covered in shining jewels. 'They must be the Sleih.'

'I hope they're not all like the rider who tried to run me down,' Mark said. 'He didn't seem the type who'd listen to the likes of us.'

'He's not the one we have to worry about.'

They stood silently, taking in this new strangeness.

The cobbled road wound its way up a steep hill like an overgrown spiral staircase. Narrow lanes went off in all directions, up and down and across the hill. Sleih in flowing, vivid gowns or wide trousers, gathered in small groups, chatting and laughing. Madach dressed more plainly in sober coloured breeches and crisp shirts with high collars, hurried in and out of elegant buildings with their arms piled with papers. There were also farmers with laden carts, people pushing barrows, women hurrying along with baskets of food, and children skipping between the grown-ups.

Up ahead, market stalls lined the lanes. Good smells came from some of the stalls. Others showed off clothing or overflowed with all kinds of things, useful and decorative.

Gwen pointed to a creamy yellow stone tower standing at the top of the city. 'That must be the King's Tower Melthrop told us about.'

The tower was hung about with coloured flags and pennants. A green flag with a silver tree symbol fluttered languidly above them all.

They set off up the winding road, which rose gently, making the distance to the tower much further than Mark first believed. All along the way, the throng of busy people continued. As they got higher, he noticed there were fewer Madach and the Sleih were more grand than those in the lower part of the Citadel. Many of the women had servants walking behind them, carrying their shopping. The servants stared at Mark and Gwen. Mark kept his head down.

'I don't think we fit in here.' He glanced at Gwen's patched clothing and dust-streaked face.

'Ignore them. We don't want to be thrown out before we even reach the King's Tower.'

They trudged on and upwards. Mark was certain the yellow

tower was getting no nearer when they came around a curve in the road and there it was, high and huge above them. The first thing Mark saw was a pair of wide and elaborate iron gates. They were closed, guarded by soldiers whose swords hung nearly to the ground.

A wide square of multi-coloured stone lay between Mark and Gwen and the iron gates.

'What a beautiful place.' Gwen gazed around the square. 'Such pretty fountains, and all those tubs full of flowers. Ma would love this.'

'Yes,' Mark said. 'I'm thinking more about those soldiers though.' He waved at the gates. 'Do you think they'll let us in?'

The soldiers paid them no attention – unlike the finely dressed Sleih ladies resting from the heat on stone benches. Judging by the little smiles and shakes of their heads, the ladies' chattering seemed directed at Mark and Gwen. Servants stood nearby, arms full of parcels. They gossiped too, and cast wrinkle-browed glances at the grubby children in the beautiful square.

'What should we do?' Mark felt like a piece of charred wood sullying fresh snow.

'I suppose we have to see if the soldiers will let us in.' Gwen frowned, and stayed where she was.

'There might be another, smaller, entrance,' Mark said.

'This looks like the main gate, so let's try here first.'

Mark watched, admiring her courage, as Gwen marched past the ladies and their frowning servants. He followed, blushing at the smothered laughter behind him.

'Well, young lady.' A soldier took a step forward to meet Gwen. 'What can I do for you today? Lost, are you?'

'No sir,' Gwen said. 'We're not lost. We've come a long, long way to see the king of the Sleih and ask for his help for our people.'

'And who are your people?'

'We are the Danae,' Mark said. He lifted his chin, eyes on the soldier. 'We are the Danae who live in the Forest. Once upon a time the Sleih helped us. We need your help again.'

There was a loud burst of tittering from the ladies seated on the benches.

Mark's blushes deepened.

'Ah,' the soldier said. 'The game today is fairytale Danae!' He chuckled. 'Haven't heard about them for a long time. You youngsters have good imaginations.'

'We are Danae,' Mark said. 'We're not a fairytale, we're real.'

'And we're serious about needing the help of the Sleih,' Gwen said. 'Madach have come from across the sea and are cutting down the Forest. We believe they'll drive us out, like they did before.'

'Oooh, it's the Nasty Madach game, is it?' The soldier winked at his fellow guard.

'It's not a game.' Gwen huffed. 'I know you think the Danae are a fairytale. We're not, we do exist.' She opened her arms wide. 'Look at us, see?'

The soldier had lost interest. Two Sleih lords riding tall prancing horses with prettily painted hooves and coloured braids in their manes, approached the gates.

The soldier shoo'd Gwen and Mark away. 'Off you go, and stop bothering important people with your games.'

He hurried back to his position, standing straight with his sword held upwards in a salute. The gates swung inwards. The Sleih lords rode through.

Chapter Twenty Eight

Trespass In The King's Tower

Gwen kept her head high as she walked from the gates. She dared not risk meeting the eyes of the pretty Sleih ladies who smiled at her and Mark, as if, Gwen sighed, they were a pair of children escaped from their ma for a day. Once they were out of sight of the gates and the square, she slumped onto the nearest step. Mark sank down too.

Gwen thought about the silver tree on the green flag and Verian's warning. Silver. Help or hindrance? In this case, no help at all.

She groaned. 'All this way and we can't see the king, let alone ask for his help.' She put her head in her hands. 'We'll have to find our way home, somehow, hope they're all there, and safe.'

'No, no, no,' Mark said. 'We can't give up this easily.'

He stood up.

'There must be another way in somewhere.'

'And you think the guards will believe us there?'

'I'm not talking about a way in with guards.'

Gwen wasn't sure about this. She followed Mark back to the square anyway. This time, instead of crossing it, Mark led the way around its edge. The pretty ladies and their servants smiled and waved.

Mark, his face pink, waved back. Gwen blushed too, and didn't wave.

The square ended in a wide garden bed hard against the yellow tower walls. Mark ducked behind a bush laden with white flowers and humming with bees.

Gwen glanced at the Sleih ladies. They'd lost interest in her and Mark and were gossiping among themselves. She slipped in after Mark.

The garden bed went on, and on, all the way to the corner, where the tower wall bulged out into a round turret.

There was no gate along the wall, nor in the turret.

'This is hopeless,' Gwen said.

'We've only come along one wall,' Mark said. 'Come on, let's see how far this garden goes.'

It went along the next wall too, to the next turret.

'There!' Mark was triumphant. 'I told you there'd be another way in.'

He put his hand on the iron handle of a narrow wooden door in the turret wall, pushed at it, leaned heavily, and fell inside.

'Oof,' he said, scrambling up.

Gwen leaned around Mark to look into a dark circular space. It was enclosed except for a slim opening, partially blocked by a cascade of blue flowers, directly opposite. Squinting in the dim light, she made out a wooden floor above her with shadowy steps spiralling into darkness through an open hatch.

Mark had darted across the space to peek around the blue flowers.

'It's all clear,' he whispered.

Gwen joined him, her heart hammering at this trespass.

Not far ahead was a lawn edged with flowers and crossed by a stone-paved path. At the intersection of the paths, a fountain glistening with moss gushed water from the mouth of a strange although familiar creature.

'A gryphon fountain,' Gwen murmured. She wondered sadly where her own tiny gryphon might be.

They looked and listened a while longer. There were no voices, no footsteps. Nothing except the splashing of the fountain.

'What do we do now?' Gwen said.

'Find the king of the Sleih.' Mark grinned.

'You think it'll be so easy?'

'Let's see.'

Mark wriggled past the blue flowers and strode down the path to the fountain as if he walked it every day.

Gwen held back, biting her lip.

'You there! Where do you think you're going?'

Gwen jumped. The shout was very close. Mark twisted around and stared up.

A rustling sounded in the floor above Gwen. A foot poked through the hatch, searching for a step.

Gwen dived for the turret door. She swung around it and pulled it almost closed. She peeked around the edge.

A guard dashed through the shadows and onto the lawn.

'Stop! In the name of the King!'

Gwen's already hammering heart pounded harder.

She waited. No one else came down the steps. Gwen ran back to the opening.

Mark was running across the lawn, away from the turret. His bag with its remains of Dorothy's food banged against his back.

The guard ran too. 'Stop!'

'Run, Mark, run.' Gwen clenched her teeth.

Though where could he run to?

The guard pulled a horn from a pouch by his side and blew it, high and loud. Guards poured from all directions. Mark was forced to a halt, his back to the gryphon fountain, surrounded by Sleih with spears and swords.

No! Gwen pushed aside the cascade of flowers, ready to face the guards alongside her brother. Through a gap in the wall of guards, Gwen saw Mark shake his head wildly. Gwen paused.

He's frightened, she thought, and took a step beyond the opening. Mark jumped up and down. The head-shaking grew more violent.

No. He was telling her, No.

Gwen stepped back into the darker space of the turret.

Two guards marched Mark across the lawn. Not back to the turret, as if they would pitch him out of the Tower's grounds – they marched him further in, down a gravelled path and around the corner of a squat, windowless building.

Two more guards headed in Gwen's direction.

She darted back to the door, slipped through and leaned on it, listening.

'How many times do we have to tell him to make sure this door is locked?' one of the guards complained.

'The next time it happens we'll have to tell the captain, which'll mean trouble.'

The first guard gave out a long sigh. 'All the urchins in the Citadel will know about this open door once the boy is free.'

'Yes.' The second guard sniggered. 'Unless we make it very clear any mention of occasional open doors carries with it painful punishments.'

The first guard snorted. 'Poor kid.'

Visions of beatings and worse filled Gwen's head. She was about to shout and demand to be arrested too when the heavy door was pushed shut. She fell against it, heard a key turning in the lock on the other side and by the time she'd gathered her wits, the laughter and chatter of the departing guards drowned out her pleas to be let back in.

Gwen's stomach churned. She ran back to the square. It was empty, save for the soldiers at the gates.

'You.' The soldier who'd shoo'd them away last time shook his head.

'Yes, me.'

Although the afternoon was moving into evening, the sun beat hotly down. Gwen's head felt light and her heart heavy.

'Still playing at Danae and Madach?' the soldier said.

'We weren't playing.' Gwen gulped. She wouldn't cry. 'We are true Danae and we do need to talk with your king.'

'Where's the other one, the boy?'

'That's what I came about.'

'Well, what is it?'

'Your guards have him.' Sobs threatened. Gwen shut them down. 'We found an open door, in the turret over there.' She waved.

'Go on.'

'We went in, or rather, Mark went in, and he ... he was caught.'

'Serves him well. He shouldn't have trespassed in the King's Tower, should he?'

'No.' Gwen stared into the soldier's eyes. 'What will happen to him, please? Can I see him?'

'Happen to him? He'll be charged with trespass and have to go before the King's Justice.' The soldier wagged his finger. 'And no, you can't see him. Not allowed, not until he's in the King's Court. You can go there, if you ask beforehand.'

'How do I ...?'

The guard's attention was distracted by a group of Sleih lords and ladies making their noisy, merry way across the square.

'Off you go, no more questions.' He flapped his hand at Gwen. 'You'll see your brother some time.'

The lords and ladies trotted through the gates. A few looked curiously at Gwen. Gwen cringed. She was dusty and tattered and close to tears. Not wanting to cry in front of these proud-looking Sleih, she hurried away, across the square down into the Citadel.

Chapter Twenty Nine

Lady Elizabeth

'You can't have your picnic there.'

Gwen glanced up from her seat on the doorstep. The doorstep belonged to a building whose sign proclaimed it to be the *Office of AG Manath, Scribe and Attorney*. Gwen had assumed AG Manath would be at home having his supper. It appeared not.

A neat Madach in a crisp shirt and carrying a pile of papers, glared down at her. Gwen bundled up Dorothy's cheese and dark bread, stuffed them into her bag and wearily rose from her seat.

She glanced back once to see the Madach watching her go, tapping his well-shod foot.

Twilight had not slowed the Citadel's busyness, with the lanes and stalls as lively as during the day. Torches hung high on the walls to light the cobbled road. Multi-coloured lanterns flickered above the stalls. With the noise and the lights it was like a party.

Gwen wandered along, barely taking in the sights and smells and sounds. She wasn't at all in a party mood.

What were the soldiers doing to Mark? Was he frightened? Were they hurting him?

And, where would she herself sleep tonight?

As Gwen walked, she cast about as if expecting a bed to pop up in the cobbled road.

And glimpsed, in a busy alley to her right, a head of golden curls standing out from the black hair of the Sleih and the duller browns and reds of the Madach.

Gwen's sudden stop in the middle of the road earned her a shove from an irate Madach woman. Gwen stared, watching the golden head, trying to be certain.

'Lucy!' Gwen stood on tiptoes and waved. 'Lucy, here, over here!'

People all around tut-tutted at this loud behaviour.

Gwen didn't care or even see. She ran to Lucy, her despair turning to joy.

Her mother was right all along. Lucy was here, with the Sleih.

'Lucy, Lucy!' Gwen dodged between the shoppers. They avoided her as if she was a rabid dog.

Lucy paid Gwen no attention. She was holding a necklace up to the light of a lantern. Her tall hat trailed a translucent material which floated in the breeze like a pale rainbow. Her deep green dress, colourful embroidery sparkling around the hem, fell in soft folds to the ground.

'Lucy, Lucy, it's me! I've found you!'

Gwen ran, marvelling at how grand her sister had become.

'We were sure you'd been kidnapped by Madach robbers and sold! But you're here!'

Gwen waited for Lucy to throw down the necklace, laugh out loud and rush to her, arms open for a hug.

Lucy didn't do that. She glanced at the noisy girl, saw she was racing right at her, opened her blue eyes wide and looked wildly about. She backed away, banging her hip on the edge of the stall.

A patrolling soldier waved his sword at Gwen. 'Off you go!' he ordered. 'Leave Lady Elizabeth alone! Who do you think you are?'

Gwen, panting from the running, stopped. She frowned.

Lucy stared, with no hint of recognition at all. The soldier had called her Lady Elizabeth.

Wasn't it Lucy? The blue depths of the young woman's eyes, the golden, curling hair – yes, it was Lucy. Although, her eyes had lost something. The liveliness which Gwen knew was gone, replaced with a most un-Lucy like blankness.

Gwen calmed herself. 'Lucy,' she said, 'it's me, Gwen, your sister. Remember? Remember Ma and Da and our village and the Forest?'

Lucy regarded Gwen with her sadly blank expression. A slight crease wrinkled her forehead, fleeing as quickly as it had come.

'I am not Lucy. I am not anyone's sister. I am Elizabeth, Lady of the Citadel of Ilatias, and,' addressing nearby shoppers in a haughty tone, 'I have no idea who this grimy urchin is.'

'Shall I run her out of the Citadel, my lady?' The soldier appeared as if he would enjoy running Gwen out of the Citadel.

'Yes,' Lucy said, to Gwen's horror. 'No, wait. She's merely a child after all.' She studied Gwen closely, shuddering delicately at her patched trousers and cloak, her trodden down boots. 'And it seems the poor girl has no parents to care for her, or teach her how to behave.' She reached up a slim hand to push back her golden curls. 'What did you say your name was, girl?'

Gwen wanted to shout, 'Wake up! What's going on here?'

Instead she said, 'Gwen. My lady. I'm your sister, and we're from the Forest. Our parents are Meg and Bob Godwin, the fisherman, although our father drowned at sea last year. And not long after, you, my sister Lucy, disappeared into the Forest.'

Lucy drew her delicate eyebrows together. 'Forest? There's no forest near here. Sorry as I am for the loss of your father and sister, I cannot help you with your Lucy.'

She turned her back on Gwen and walked away. By this time, the onlookers had gone back to their shopping, apparently

155

losing interest when the soldier was not allowed to run the ragamuffin girl out of the Citadel.

Gwen, in a panic that she might not find Lucy again, called out the first thing which came into her head.

'We have another sister too. Callie. Callie misses Lucy dreadfully.'

Lucy stopped, shaking her head as if trying to clear a fogginess inside. Gwen waited. Whether it was Callie's name, or another reason, Lucy glanced over her shoulder.

'Come with me,' she said, and continued to walk down the alley.

Gwen gave a long sigh and ran to catch up.

They climbed the cobbled road for a short distance until Lucy made her way up a set of broad stone steps to a door which opened as she approached. She led Gwen inside.

Gwen's mouth fell open at the splendour she saw.

The floor of the spacious hall was laid with a white, shiny stone shot through with thin veins of pink, the walls were the same soft yellow stone as the Tower, and the high ceiling was painted the palest blue, with floating silver clouds and jewelled birds flying across it.

Wide and tall mirrors hung between the many doors leading off to the right and left. There were pictures too, showing graceful folk singing, feasting and dancing. From somewhere inside, Gwen could hear water trickling. The cool and refreshing noise blended gently with the lilting notes of music playing in a distant room.

Gwen was horribly aware of her grimy face and dusty clothes. No wonder the soldiers sent her and Mark away. They were as tattered and filthy as beggars, or robber children.

A young Madach woman wearing a white apron over a grey dress and with her brown hair pinned beneath a white cap, stood in the hallway. She took a step backwards when she saw Gwen.

'My lady, where has this person come from? Why is she

here? Does His Highness know of this?'

'She says she comes from the forest, wherever the forest may be. She seems to be confused, and I think it's because she's lost,' Lucy said.

'Girl,' she said to Gwen, 'this is Coral. She will show you where you can bathe and we can dispose of those clothes.'

Lucy's nose lifted, in the same way it lifted at home when Callie arrived in the cottage smelling of mud and wet leaves.

'Afterwards we can eat, and talk some more, because I'm curious about your story and why you think I am this Lucy when I'm clearly not.'

Coral opened her mouth to protest, but Lucy had already disappeared through one of the many doors.

'Well, if anything goes missing,' Coral said, 'we'll know who to blame, won't we? Fancy bringing the likes of you in here. Leave your bag there and come along. You certainly do need a bath. We'll have to see what the prince has to say about all this. Not pleased, I wouldn't think.'

Prince? What did Coral mean? Would Gwen be able to talk to someone important, after all?

Chapter Thirty

An Arrogant Prince

Gwen's frustration threatened to spill over into anger.

Earlier, the fresh feeling from the bath and the clean red silk shirt and blue cotton skirt Lucy had given her to wear had lifted her spirits. She'd been confident that once she'd had a chance to talk properly with Lucy she would say, 'Oh yes, of course I remember!' and be Lucy again.

Now, sitting at the long, polished table with the remains of their meal before them, Gwen felt low all over again.

Despite saying she was curious about Gwen's story, Lucy showed barely any interest in hearing about the Danae villages and their family in the Forest. Mention of Callie had brought about a slight widening of her eyes, encouraging Gwen to talk more about her little sister. Lucy was not to be drawn.

'She sounds sweet,' was all she would say.

She was also dismissive about Mark when Gwen told her about the Tower.

'I'm sorry your brother is in the king's prison. He should not have trespassed, you know.'

'Can you help him?'

'No, I cannot. He will need to wait his turn for the King's Justice.'

'Coral said something about the prince,' Gwen said. 'Do you know him? Would you be able to help me see the king, before Mark has to face this Justice?'

Lucy stared past Gwen. 'Yes, I know the prince,' she said in a colourless voice. 'He's been kind to me. But I could not ask such a favour of him. It's not my place to ask favours.'

She was silent for a time, before tapping the table and demanding Gwen go on with her story.

Gwen wanted to talk about the prince and the king and was about to ask, Why can't you ask favours? when Coral hurried into the room. She curtsied, and in hushed, reverential tones, said, 'Prince Elrane has come, my lady, to see you and your visitor.'

Lucy jumped from her chair and faced the door. She clasped her hands in front of her like a little girl. She didn't smile.

Gwen's curiosity turned to uneasiness. She hadn't met him yet, but she already disliked this prince who had now followed Coral into the room.

'My dear lady, I hope I find you well?' The prince took hold of Lucy's clasped hands.

Lucy curtsied and said yes, she was well and it was kind of His Highness to think of her and to visit. Would His Highness care for a glass of something cool to drink, as it was indeed warm out despite the evening air?

The prince declined the drink, dropped Lucy's hands and walked up to Gwen. He examined her like she was a horse he was thinking of buying.

Gwen stared back. The prince was handsome, true. But the effect of his straight nose, clear golden skin and lustrous black hair was spoilt by a sulkiness about his green eyes and full mouth. It was as if no one had ever told him No.

'I heard you had kindly taken in a ragged young girl,' the prince said to Lucy.

Lucy twisted her fingers together.

'Not so ragged now.' The prince raised his fine dark eyebrows. 'All scrubbed up I see.' He took in the table's empty plates. 'Well fed too.'

He smiled at Lucy, as one would smile at a cutely mischievous toddler. 'You're such a sweet, good person, Elizabeth,' he said gently. 'You shouldn't put yourself to trouble like this. I'm sure the girl would be well cared for at the home for lost and orphaned children. Why don't you have Coral take her there?'

'If you think it best, Highness,' Lucy said.

Gwen drew in a sharp breath.

Lucy dropped her gaze to the floor. 'Although I hoped she might be a good companion for me, at least for a while,' she said. 'She has stories of an old man living in a forest a long way from here, who seems to have Sleih powers. I would like to hear more of her adventures and,' she raised her eyes to the prince, 'it's lonely here sometimes. Please let her stay, at least for a short time?'

The prince drew his brows together at this speech. He turned to Gwen.

'What are you called? And why are you here in the Citadel of Ilatias?'

Gwen couldn't say she was Lucy's sister, not when Lucy would deny it.

'I'm Gwen Godwin, from the Forest, by the edge of the sea. It's a long way from here, as Lady Elizabeth says. Me and my brother, Mark, have spent many weeks on our journey.'

The prince pulled out a chair, sat down. 'Brother? Where's he?'

'Yes, my brother.' Gwen paused. Lucy, behind the prince, was giving tiny shakes of her head.

Too bad.

'We went to the gates of the King's Tower,' Gwen said, 'because we need to see the king, and when the soldiers wouldn't let us in Mark found another door, in a turret. He went into the grounds and the guards arrested him. I don't know where he is and everyone says he'll have to wait for the King's Justice.' She bit her lip. 'He only did it because we need to see the king.'

Lucy interrupted. 'I told the girl her brother should not have trespassed in the King's Tower and he must pay the penalty.'

'Absolutely.' The prince nodded at Lucy, who blushed.

Gwen stopped herself from rolling her eyes. She waited for the prince to ask why they needed to see the king. He didn't, so Gwen told him anyway.

'You see, Your Highness, our Forest is in danger, and our people, the Danae, may be in danger too. The Danae believe the Sleih helped us once before, and me and Mark have travelled from the Forest to plead before the king, to ask if the Sleih will help us this time.'

The prince's eyes narrowed. 'Danae, as in the old tales?'

'Fairytale Danae?' Lucy giggled.

The prince's gaze shifted back to Lucy, who stopped giggling and blushed pinker.

Gwen was curious as to why the prince seemed worried, or upset, nervous, whenever he looked at Lucy.

'Yes, Danae', she said. 'We're not a fairytale. And my brother is locked up and he hasn't done anything except try to plead for help for our people, and we have to wait for this King's Justice to see if he'll be freed and there's no one to help us, no one at all.'

The prince was politely cool. 'As you say, the Forest is a long way from here. I don't see why the Sleih would help your people. Danae or not.'

Gwen's heart sank.

'What about Mark? Can you help him?'

'Help him? A trespasser?'

The prince rose from his chair.

'My lady,' he said to Lucy, 'I do not think you should be harbouring the sister of a trespasser, whatever his apparent motive was.'

He again peered intently at Gwen, although he spoke to

Lucy. 'The Danae are a mythical race, and even if they did exist once it's impossible there are any with us today. I urge you to send this girl away, before something happens you may regret.'

Lucy twisted her fingers more tightly. 'Yes, yes of course, Your Highness, I understand. I apologise for my foolishness.'

The prince smiled his condescending smile and held Lucy's hands. 'Never foolish, my dear Elizabeth. Merely too kind and too generous.'

He took no more notice of Gwen, said goodbye to Lucy and left the room. Coral scurried down the hall to see him out.

Chapter Thirty One

An Orphanage And A Prison

'Lucy, what's wrong with you? That awful prince treats you like a pet puppy.'

Gwen wanted to shake her sister and punch smug Prince Elrane all at the same time. Given the prince had gone, she was left with dealing with Lucy, who had returned to her seat and was idly playing with an empty glass.

'I am not Lucy.' Lucy banged the glass down. Much the way the real Lucy would have done.

'Then who are you? Who is Lady Elizabeth and where is your family?'

'Ah, I have no family. My family were,' Lucy hesitated, 'killed. In a raid by robber Madach. I escaped and Prince Elrane found me wandering in a wood, not remembering the awful things which had happened.' She tilted the glass back and forth, staring at it. 'Since that terrible time the prince has been kind to me. He makes sure I lack for nothing. He tells me it is best if I don't remember.'

Gwen felt any argument against this tale would be a waste of time. In any case, Coral was back in the room with Gwen's bag in her hand.

'Lady Elizabeth, I need to take the girl to the home for orphans immediately, before they close their doors for the night.'

Gwen backed away from Coral's outstretched hand.

'No!' she appealed to Lucy. 'Please, you mustn't send me there. How will I be able to do anything for Mark or see the king, if I'm shut up in a home?'

Lucy looked from Gwen to Coral. Coral's chin jutted out as if she was prepared to defend to the death the prince's request.

'Why not simply let me go?' Gwen said.

'No.' Lucy sighed. 'You mustn't wander the streets this late.' She nodded slowly, as if her mind was made up. 'Of course you must go to the home. For your own protection.'

Coral took tight hold of Gwen's hand. 'Come along.' She pulled Gwen down the hall and out of the house.

Gwen fought Coral's strong grip. 'Lucy, don't do this!'

Lucy watched from the front door. Her eyes were blank. Her fingers picked at the silk cloth of her skirt.

'Please!' Gwen begged from the bottom of the steps.

Lucy gave her head a quick shake and walked back into the house. She closed the door.

Angry humiliation raged in Gwen's chest. How dare Lucy treat her like this?

But it wasn't really Lucy. The thought gave Gwen small comfort.

Coral marched across Ilatias, eyes fixed forward, ignoring Gwen's pleas to be let loose. Gwen tried appealing to the few passers-by. They pretended to neither see nor hear.

Coral finally stopped in front of a tall building with many high, barred – and dark – windows. She dragged Gwen up the steps and banged the heavy knocker, which was shaped like a crying child's head.

They waited, Gwen squirming, Coral tightening her grip.

A thin Madach woman with hair untidily plaited down her back opened the door. She tugged at the shawl wrapped around her nightdress and squinted at Coral down her sharp nose.

'What is it? Can't it wait 'til morning? We're closed for the night.' The woman made to shut the door.

Coral pushed it open. 'I've an order from Prince Elrane. He requires you to take this young girl in, for her safety.'

The woman huffed. 'No beds left.'

'His Highness will pay of course,' Coral said.

The woman eyed Gwen. 'Won't take up much room, will she?'

She opened the door wider. Coral loosened her grasp on Gwen to hand her to the woman.

Gwen saw her chance. She twisted hard, wrenched herself free and took the steps two at a time, stumbling into the road.

She picked herself up, heard Coral shout, followed by the slamming of the orphanage door.

Gwen raced to the nearest lighted alleyway, hoping to lose any pursuit among late night shoppers. She skidded around a corner and fell over a man propped against the wall. Whatever was in the mug in his hand slopped all over his shirt.

'Hey, watcha think you're doing?'

Gwen didn't stop. With thudding heart, she dodged around a Madach arguing loudly with a gaudily dressed Sleih woman and found she had to slow her flight to wind between the rowdy crowd which spilled out of well-lit taverns into the lane, drinking, laughing and talking.

An old woman sitting on a bench stood up suddenly in Gwen's way. Gwen careened into her, muttered, 'Sorry, sorry,' and kept going.

'Pickpocket, thief!' the woman yelled.

Gwen searched desperately for a way out, saw a darker lane off to her right and with a glance behind her, sped down it. At another turning, she stopped briefly to take in gulps of air before hurrying on. A cat running out from the shadows sent her heart thumping harder.

She ran, skittering around a pile of stinking rubbish, swivelling her head from side to side to spot anything else which might be hovering in the dark corners.

The lane ended in a wide covered space. Gwen stopped at its edge, her hand pressed to a wooden upright, catching her breath. In the dim light offered by a few scattered lanterns, she made out rows of tables, some piled with items hidden under cloths, others empty, many with wooden boxes underneath them.

A market.

No one was there to see Gwen crawl under a table where the cloth hung to the ground. She slumped against a sturdy table leg and drew her trembling knees up to her chest. Her breathing and her heart slowed.

What was happening to Mark? she worried. Gwen imagined her brother in a cold cell, sleeping on a hard, damp floor and being tossed a mouldy crust once a day.

And poor, poor Lucy. Whatever was wrong with her?

Tears gathered.

It had all gone wrong. They had come all this way for nothing.

Gwen rested her head on her knees and cried herself into an exhausted sleep.

***

Mark lay on his back on the prickly straw mattress. A moonbeam shining through the high window sliced the darkness of his cell.

What was happening to Gwen? he fretted. And what would happen to him?

The guard had said, as he locked the iron door, 'It's the King's Justice for you, lad. Serious too, trespassing in the King's Tower.'

'I need to see the king, I need to talk to him,' Mark had said.

'Oh, you'll see the king. No problem.' The guard had chuckled.

Mark closed his eyes. Sleep, he told himself. See what

166

happens tomorrow.

'Your Highness, what brings you down to the Tower Cells?' The guard's voice came clearly through the door.

'Do you have a young boy here, name of Mark Godwin?' a haughty voice said.

Mark forgot about sleeping. He leaned up on one elbow.

'Yes, Highness, we do indeed. How did Your Highness come to know of this boy?'

'That is no matter for you.'

'Of course, Your Highness.' A pause. 'Umm, what did you want with the boy, Highness?'

His Highness took his time responding. Finally he said, 'I wish to talk with him. Bring him here.'

The key rattled in the lock of Mark's cell door. The guard pushed it open. 'You have an important visitor, lad. Prince Elrane himself. Make sure you behave, eh?'

Mark hopped off the mattress and followed the guard, curious to meet his important visitor.

The prince sat on a bench at a wooden table. 'Sit down,' he said. He waved at the bench opposite.

Mark obeyed. 'How do you know my name and how did you know I was here and why do you want to talk to me?'

The prince lifted an eyebrow. 'One question at a time, I think.' He searched Mark's face and Mark found himself staring into eyes the colour of the green waves which washed against the cliffs below the Forest. They reminded him of Callie's eyes.

'Before I answer,' the prince said, not taking his green eyes off Mark's face, 'I have questions for you.'

'What questions?'

'Who are you and where are you from?'

'I'm Mark, Mark Godwin, from the Forest, and I have to see the king.'

'Why are you here in the Citadel of Ilatias?'

'To see the king, like I said, and ask for his help for our people.'

'Who are your people?' The green eyes held Mark's gaze.

'We are the Danae of The Forest,' Mark said, 'and Madach have come from across the oceans to cut down our trees and me and my sister, Gwen, have come all this way to find the Sleih, although everyone thinks the Sleih are an old myth. We have to ask the king for help.' A thought occurred to him. 'Have you seen Gwen? Has Gwen sent you here?'

The prince let Mark's gaze go. He studied the table top. 'Yes, I have seen Gwen,' came his curt answer.

'Is she all right? Is she safe?'

'Yes, she's safe.'

Mark blew out his cheeks. He was about to ask where Gwen was and how she'd found the prince, when the prince said, 'We believe the Danae are a fairytale.'

'No.' Mark shook his head. 'We were wrong about the Sleih and you're wrong about the Danae.'

He stood up, twirled around. 'Do I look like a Madach? I'm too small, aren't I?'

The prince gave a brief and humourless smile.

'When we found out the Madach thought we were a fairytale, we had to be careful not to tell anyone we were Danae because we got caught by robbers and they wanted to sell us, as fairytale slaves,' Mark said.

'Yes, I can see the value robbers would place on having fairytale slaves to sell.'

Mark sighed deeply. 'Our sister Lucy might have been kidnapped by robbers, in the spring. She was picking wild garlic and disappeared. The searchers found her basket. And hoof prints which didn't go anywhere.'

The prince's eyebrows rose and fell. His sea-green eyes darkened. 'Picking wild garlic?'

'Yes.' Mark thought it a strange thing to mention out of all the things he'd talked about. 'And Lucy would be easy to sell, because Ma always says she's the prettiest girl in the village, all golden curls and big blue eyes. Can never see it myself.'

'Golden curls and blue eyes?'

'Yes. As I said, easy to sell, I suppose.'

'Ah.' The prince gazed into Mark's eyes for a few more seconds. Then he leaned back on the bench and blinked as if waking from a heavy sleep.

Mark blinked too. He was so tired.

'You may take the boy back to his cell,' the prince said to the guard.

'Wait.' Mark forgot his tiredness. 'You haven't answered my questions.'

'Gwen is safe, which is all you need to know.'

The prince, ignoring Mark's rushed questions, walked quickly away, his pale golden forehead creased.

Mark wondered if the prince would visit him again.

Chapter Thirty Two

Lost And Found

Thud!

Something heavy thumped onto the table above Gwen. She woke with a start, and remembered where she was. She stretched her stiff legs and shoulders, listening to the din of people talking and shouting beyond her hiding place.

Thud!

Gwen winced and painfully rose to her hands and knees. She tugged aside the cloth covering the table and peeked through the narrow crack. What she saw was a collection of moving legs in boots, squeaking barrow wheels, and boxes being dragged along the floor.

The thuds above her stopped. Gwen dared lift the cloth higher.

'Hey, what you doing under there? You street urchins! You know you're not allowed in here!'

Gwen slid out from under the table, struggled upright and fled further into the market. It was filling with early morning shoppers and the stallholders were too busy to bother about a street urchin, as long as she didn't come near their goods. She wandered among the stalls, trying not to get in anybody's way and thinking what she should do. Go back to Lucy? She was likely to end up in the orphanage. Go back to the Tower gates? Get herself arrested, like Mark. At least they'd be together.

A cry of 'Hot pies! Start the day with a hot pie!' cut into

Gwen's worrying.

Pies?

Melthrop Kaine! Of course. Melthrop might be here.

The pie seller wasn't Melthrop. Nor was the next one. But Gwen had a purpose now. She marched up and down the crowded aisles lined with food sellers of all kinds, searching out the one pie seller she wanted to see.

Her search took her deeper into the market with no success. Gwen grew anxious. Melthrop could easily be selling his pies in another town.

The food stalls were thinning, there was only one more aisle to search.

It was no good. He wasn't in the market. Not today.

She turned the last corner ... and there he was, holding a steaming pie out to a brawny Madach farmer.

***

Lady Melda paused in the process of taking off her blue silk cloak. She had just returned home from her fruitless trip to the robber Madach camp, her rage festering all the way back to Ilatias.

This Chester and his ragbag of people would long remember the foolishness of not keeping their promises to a Lady of the Sleih, especially a Seer.

But now an image stirred in her mind, strong enough to distract her. It was an image of two children, faceless, yet familiar.

Such strong auras. She recalled the cage and the tent where her Danae had been held, briefly. They must be here, in Ilatias.

Lady Melda threw her cloak at the waiting servant. 'I will not be disturbed, not for anything.' She took the stairs quickly.

In her solar, Lady Melda stood unmoving in the middle of the book-lined room. She cast her mind back to the Madach camp. First she concentrated on the willow cage where the boy had been unsatisfactorily imprisoned. Then she brought her mind to the tent where the girl had been held. She pushed aside the image of the red-headed Madach girl to focus on the Danae aura left within the stained hide walls.

The faceless image rose before her. They were indeed close. The aura locked with the image – the girl, yes, she could see her, shadowy, as if in a mist. Brown hair, tanned skin, slight build.

The boy wasn't with her. Ah, there he was. This image – coppery hair, hazel eyes, thin and wiry – meshed with the aura from the willow cage.

A prison cell? What was he doing in a prison cell? The lady huffed loudly. She couldn't get to him there. It might be a good thing, though. The brat couldn't make pleas for help from a prison cell.

She thought hard about the girl. Where was she?

A market, the girl was in a market. Which market? The lady couldn't tell. She threw her hands up, muttered, 'By the Beings, how many markets are there in Ilatias?' and moved with quick grace into the hall and down the stairs.

The servant, not expecting to see her this soon, was napping in his chair.

'My cloak,' Lady Melda said. 'Hurry up.'

The servant twitched awake. He fetched the blue cloak from its silver hook, draped it over the lady's shoulders and rushed to the front door. He reached it at the same instant Lady Melda did. She pushed past him and stepped out into the sunny morning.

***

'Melthrop! It's me, Gwen. Remember me?'

Melthrop Kaine froze, his pie-laden hand outstretched to the farmer. He beamed, thrust the pie at the farmer and ignored the proffered payment.

'You found me, when I couldn't find you!'

Gwen rushed forward. 'I hoped you'd be here!'

Melthrop danced out from behind the stall to take hold of Gwen's arms.

'I am so pleased, so happy to see you, safe and not in a robber camp.' He eyed her crumpled, dirt-stained, albeit stylish, dress and blouse. 'Although it does seem you're still sleeping in your clothes.'

'Yes, I am and I'm so happy to see you too.' Gwen burst into tears.

'Gwen?' Melthrop frowned. 'What is it?' Then, 'Mark! Where's Mark? Is he still with the robbers?'

'No, no, he's here, in prison, for trespassing in the King's Tower and he has to go before the King's Justice and I don't know how to help him.'

'In prison for trespassing?'

The queue of people wanting pies for their breakfasts was getting longer and there was a good deal of foot shuffling and people muttering 'Ahem' and coughing politely.

'Stall's closed, run out of goods,' Melthrop said.

'There's lots of pies there.' A thickset labourer waved his hand over the stall.

A woman with a basket on her arm tut-tutted. 'It's early. How could you have run out?'

'All sold, have to take them to this young lady's mistress.' He tapped Gwen's shoulder. 'Hurry up, young lady. We don't want them getting cold.'

Gwen smiled through her sniffles. The queue of people melted away, grumbling, and Gwen helped Melthrop pack up his cart.

'I'm sorry to interrupt your pie-selling.'

'Nonsense. About sold out anyway,' Melthrop lied cheerfully.

He stowed away the last of the cakes, closed and locked the back of the cart and led Gwen to a table where Gwen ate the pie Melthrop had kept aside for her.

Melthrop had many questions and Gwen answered them

all. Finally, she came to the point where she'd discovered Lucy in the alley.

'I found Lucy,' she said. 'Only she's not Lucy anymore. Something's happened to her.'

'Why, it's wonderful you found your sister,' Melthrop said. 'But what's wrong with her? Is she hurt?'

'Not in her body. It's her mind.' Gwen crumpled the empty paper bag she'd used as a plate. 'She's lost all memory of us, of Ma and Da and Callie and home. She doesn't know who she is, and she's friends with a prince and when he visits she's all blushes and 'yes, Prince Elrane' and 'no, Prince Elrane'.' Gwen giggled. 'Which isn't the real Lucy at all. And she's listless and unhappy.'

'Hmm.' Melthrop gazed absently at a fishmonger struggling past with a shallow tray of splashing silver fish. 'If I didn't know better, I'd guess your sister's been bewitched.'

'Bewitched? You mean someone's put a spell on her?' Gwen found it strange to talk of such things in the busy practicality of the hustling market.

'Takes powerful Sleih magic to enchant a person, and extremely frowned on by the king and the seers.' Melthrop tapped his steepled fingers together. 'There might be another reason she's like she is, though I can't think what.'

Melthrop took Gwen's hand, smiling gently. 'At least you've found her, here, with the Sleih, and not in a robber camp or already sold as a fairytale slave.'

'Yes, you're right. I should be grateful she's safe.'

'Talking of finding things ...' Melthrop let go of Gwen's hand to reach into his shirt pocket. He pulled out a slim silver chain. 'Here,' he said, handing the chain to Gwen. 'I think this is yours.'

'Oh.' Gwen took the shiny gryphon pendant carefully. 'You found it, thank you! I was desperate when I realised I'd lost it. Josh gave it to me. It's meant to ward off evil magic.'

Gwen gazed at the pendant for a long moment. With great care, she hung it around her neck and fastened the clasp.

***

Lady Melda stopped so suddenly in the busy road that a soberly dressed Madach holding a pile of documents ran into her back. He cursed, saw she was a Sleih Seer and apologised instead.

Lady Melda felt the blood drain from her face. Her hands trembled. The misty image of the Danae girl swirled for an instant before her face, and vanished. In its place, blackness. She found she could not remember what she had seen in the images, back in her solar, nor where she believed the girl was.

Where had she been heading? If the girl was in the Citadel, she could be anywhere. Lady Melda couldn't imagine why she was tramping the streets like a servant.

She stood on the pavement, unseeing, and unaware of the people stepping around her. After a time, she slowly retraced her steps. She opened the door to her house. The servant was napping in his chair. Lady Melda ignored him. Without removing her cloak, she climbed the stairs and entered her solar, staring as one dream-walking.

The rat was waiting for her on the window-sill, gnawing a bone. It peered at her with its bright beady eyes.

Found them!

'Found them?' Lady Melda's head snapped towards the rat. 'Where, where? Tell me?'

They're in a Madach robber camp. Should be someone on his way to let you know, tell you to go fetch them.

The rat preened its fur, its tail curling down from the window sill, satisfied with a job well done.

It was most surprised therefore when its benefactor screamed, grabbed its tail and, without bothering to open the window, hurled it to the pavement in a shower of glass.

Chapter Thirty Three

Gryphon Magic

Gwen fingered the pendant and gazed at Melthrop.

'I wonder,' she said.

She ignored Melthrop's questioning look and stood up. 'I have to go back to Lucy. Will you come with me? I'll need you to persuade her not to send me to the orphans' home.'

'Yes, happy to. And afterwards I'll search out a friend of mine who might be able to help Mark. He's an attorney, name of Manath.'

'A G Manath?'

'How ...?'

'We met.' Gwen explained the brief encounter.

Melthrop chortled. 'Oh, he's not a bad man. Mustn't have had a good day.'

***

'Coral, please tell Lucy, I mean Lady Elizabeth, I have to talk to her.'

Coral opened the door a crack and pulled Gwen into the shiny-floored hall.

'Why have you come here? You know I'll have to take you to the home for lost and orphaned children.'

The door was pushed further open from the outside. Coral jumped back at the sight of the well-rounded, grey-haired Madach standing there, beaming at her.

'Who are you and why don't you knock, like other people?'

'I'm this young lady's guardian. She's not lost, nor is she an orphan. She's with me.'

'And we must see the lady,' Gwen said.

Coral glared at her, and at Melthrop Kaine.

'Why must you see me?'

Lucy came through a nearby door to frown at Gwen. She ignored Melthrop.

'Lucy, I mean my lady, this is Melthrop Kaine, a friend of mine. Mark and I met him on the road to Ilatias.'

Lucy glanced briefly at Melthrop. 'Why must you see me?' she said to Gwen.

'Can we sit down, while I explain why we've come?'

Coral waited to either close or open the door.

Gesturing languidly for Coral to shut the door, Lucy sighed. 'Very well. In here. Whatever it is you must say, be quick, and leave.'

She led them into a carpeted sitting room where she plumped listlessly onto a soft sofa so filled with fat cushions there was hardly space to sit. Gwen sat on a stool in front of Lucy.

'I want to show you this.' Gwen lifted the gryphon nestled at her neck.

'You've come back to show me a necklace?'

'Yes, I'd like you to try it on. I think it'd suit you, the blue would match your eyes.'

Gwen undid the clasp, laid the pendant in her palm and held out her hand to Lucy.

Gwen's hand twitched. Something had tickled her skin.

Lucy drew back. 'The prince was right. There's something strange about you. I want you to leave.'

Coral hovered behind her mistress, apparently willing to throw Gwen bodily into the street, and Melthrop after her.

Melthrop shifted his head from Gwen to Lucy. His forehead

was creased as if he agreed with Lucy about Gwen's odd behaviour.

Lucy made to stand up. Gwen grabbed her hand, forced it around, and dropped the chain into Lucy's palm.

Lucy gasped. 'What are you ...? Aaaggh!'

She jumped up from the sofa, scattering cushions to the floor. She stretched out her arm, waving her hand violently to throw the pendant away.

She couldn't.

Her fingers had closed around it and stayed closed however hard Lucy shook her hand.

Lucy's eyes were wide, her mouth open, ready to scream.

Gwen cried out, 'Lucy, what's happening?'

Lucy's scream came as a strangled gurgle. Her legs buckled and she dropped to the carpet. Her hand unclasped. The pendant rolled onto the floor.

Gwen fell to her knees. 'Coral, bring water, quickly.' Her stomach churned at the sight of Lucy's white face. 'Lucy, Luce, wake up, don't die!'

'She won't die.' Melthrop had pressed a finger to Lucy's neck. 'She's simply fainted. Although why, now there's a mystery.'

He squinted at Gwen who rocked back and forth on her heels, staring into Lucy's face.

A tense Coral handed Gwen a glass. Gwen lifted Lucy's head and poured water into her mouth. Lucy spluttered. Water dribbled onto her silk blouse.

Gwen bent closer. 'Lucy, Lucy, wake up.'

Lucy's eyes snapped open.

Gwen started back, spilling more water onto Lucy's face.

Lucy's vivid blue eyes glittered with anger. 'What are you trying to do, drown me?' She shook the water from her face.

Gwen's mouth opened.

Lucy's angry eyes softened. 'Gwen! What are you doing here?'

Gwen's pulse thudded. 'You know who I am?'

'Don't be silly. You're Gwen.'

The sad, washed-out listlessness of Lucy's eyes was gone. The anger was gone too.

'Shouldn't I know who you are?' Lucy sounded troubled, as if she knew there was a good reason Gwen had asked the question.

'Yes, of course you should.' Gwen gave a half-smile. She wasn't fully certain her plan had worked.

Gwen and Melthrop helped Lucy onto the sofa.

Coral poured a glass of ruby wine from a decanter and thrust it into Lucy's hand. 'Take a sip, my lady. It'll help, after the fainting.' She glowered at Gwen.

Lucy held the stem of the glass, not drinking. She shook her head.

'What's happening?' Her voice quavered, as if hearing it surprised her.

Gwen stood on the spot where Lucy had fainted.

'I think,' she said, and bit her top lip. 'I think I cured you. That you're better now.'

'Cured me?' Lucy hesitated. 'I didn't know you before? Did I? Or have you only now arrived, and me not knowing you was a dream?'

'Not a dream.' Gwen was daring to hope. 'You didn't know me. And now you do.'

'Why didn't I know you? Why are you here? When did you come?'

'We've been searching for you, and found you here, with the Sleih.'

Lucy stared. 'Searching for me?'

She drew in her breath, gradually let it out, and closed her eyes.

'Of course, the prince. It was the prince.' Tears welled, spilling over her lashes to her pink cheeks. 'I remember. The prince came, and I rode off with him, because, because ...' She sniffed loudly. 'Poor Ma, what was I thinking, to run away? How could I?'

Gwen's heart beat wildly. 'It wasn't your fault,' she said. 'You were bewitched.'

'Bewitched?'

'Yes, my lady,' Melthrop said. 'It would appear the prince made you a victim of powerful Sleih magic and brought you here to Ilatias.'

A gasp from Coral. 'No, he wouldn't. Not the prince.'

Lucy ignored Coral's protest. 'Magic? And you've cured me, Gwen?'

Gwen nodded.

Lucy stared into the ruby wine for a long time. When she raised her head she laughed.

'Come here,' she cried to Gwen. 'Let me hug you. I can't believe you're here, and thank you.'

Gwen, on her way to being hugged, spotted the pendant on the carpet. She picked it up.

'It's changed.' She showed the jewel to Melthrop.

'What's changed?' Lucy said.

The gryphon was no longer reclining sideways, one wing held close against the silver lion body, the other upright behind. It faced forward, the emerald eyes narrowed, the mouth – a tiny ruby tongue visible – open in a ferocious snarl, both wings unfurled.

Gwen laid the pendant on a low table and she and Melthrop gaped at it until Lucy said, 'Are you going to tell me what's going on?'

***

Gwen curled up in the sofa cushions by Lucy's side, listening to her story.

Lucy remembered picking wild garlic, the splendid black horse, its prettily painted hooves dancing on the forest floor, and the prince's deep eyes, holding Lucy spellbound. And

180

afterwards, life in the Citadel, an emptiness inside her, believing it all to do with the loss of her family to the robber Madach.

'Not the Madach, not this time,' Gwen said. 'I knew it was to do with that awful prince.'

'Callie was there too,' Lucy said, as if suddenly remembering.

'Callie?' Gwen shifted in the cushions. 'The prince must have cast some kind of spell on her too, because she knew nothing at all, not even going into the Forest with you that morning.'

'Is she all right?'

'Yes. Fine.'

A memory of the night she and Mark left the village came to Gwen's mind. She could see Callie's green eyes – so like these Sleih, so like the prince's eyes – searching her face, searching Mark's face, and Meg's too. How they'd all thought it the most sensible thing in the world for her and Mark to journey into the dangers of the Deep Forest, not knowing if the Sleih existed or where Lucy really was.

It had all been Callie's idea, yet they all agreed to it, easily.

Gwen whooshed out a breath. What kind of enchantment had this prince cast on Callie?

'More than fine,' she said to Lucy, and shook her head.

Lucy took Gwen's hands in hers. 'You said 'we' before. You said 'we've been searching for you.' Who else is here, and where are they?'

'Mark. But he's in the king's prison on a charge of trespassing in the King's Tower. That's where Melthrop has gone, to see someone who might be able to help.'

'Trespass?'

Gwen drew a deep breath. 'There's an awful lot to explain.'

Chapter Thirty Four

A Royal Confession

Melthrop Kaine returned in the late afternoon.

'Mark is comfortable enough,' he said. 'They're treating him well, given he appears to have friends in high places.'

Before Gwen could ask, What friends? Melthrop said, 'Prince Elrane visited Mark yesterday evening.'

'Prince Elrane?' Gwen said. 'What was he up to, visiting Mark?'

'Who can tell the ways of princes,' Melthrop said solemnly. 'In any case, the important news is that Mark will appear before the King's Justice tomorrow at noon. My friend Manath tells me you can attend, Gwen, as his sister.'

'And me?' Lucy said.

'Prince Elrane has requested the presence of the Lady Elizabeth also,' Melthrop said with a smirk.

'What's it to do with the prince?'

'Why, didn't I say?' The smirk deepened. 'Prince Elrane has declared he will speak for Mark.'

***

Gwen and Lucy waited with the brightly dressed courtiers in the king's throne room. The king – a slender, elegant Sleih of middle age, clean-shaven and with long hair as black and shiny as a raven's wing held back by a silver circlet – was pronouncing his Justice on a young Madach man. Beside the king, a delicate

Sleih woman dressed in green and silver studied the young man as intently as her husband did.

Gwen gazed around the light-filled room. Its length was marked by pillars of dark wood stretching to the vaulted roof like sturdy tree trunks. Carved leafy strands twisted around the pillars, with gloriously jewelled birds and butterflies perched in the leaves, ready for flight. High in the sand-coloured walls, stone-worked boughs arched gracefully over windows sparkling with a translucent blue light. Were these Josh's fabled diamond windows?

It was a stylised forest, graceful and light. Gwen imagined a soft breeze passing through, rustling the leaves and the feathers of the birds. It was colourful and beautiful and, despite its awe-inspiring richness, welcoming.

It wasn't like her Forest, though, Gwen decided, missing home with a sudden deep longing.

The young Madach man rose, bowed to the king and the queen, and was led out through a door behind the thrones.

A moment of chatter was silenced by a short blast on a trumpet. A herald announced, 'Master Mark Godwin of the Forest is brought before King Ieldon, King of the Sleih, to meet the King's Justice.'

A Sleih dressed in unusually sober clothes and standing by the king's throne ('The King's Secretary,' Lucy whispered), asked, 'On what charge is Master Godwin brought before the King's Justice?'

The herald consulted a long sheet of paper. 'Trespass in the King's Tower.'

The King's Secretary said, 'Who defends Master Godwin?'

The herald went back to his paper, screwed up his eyes as if he wasn't certain what he was reading, and said in a less than confident voice, 'His Highness, Prince Elrane of the House of Wood.'

The king and queen exchanged looks. The queen leaned

forward, staring hard at the doors into the throne room. The courtiers and Gwen followed the queen's gaze.

Prince Elrane and Mark stepped into the room and walked the forest-green carpet which led to the dais where the king and the queen sat. Mark wore new clothes – plain brown trousers and a white shirt as befitted a prisoner. He was the cleanest Gwen had seen him in months. His copper hair shone in the sunny room.

As they neared the dais, the prince indicated to Mark he should stay where he was while he himself approached the thrones.

The prince bowed low. 'Majesties, I am here today defending this young man. First, however, I must throw myself on your majesties' mercy, through a sorry tale I have to tell.'

'What may this sorry tale be, Prince?' King Ieldon said.

The prince lowered his head, although his words carried clearly across the room. 'Sire, I have committed a great wrong and I expect my punishment to be fitting. I do not fear punishment.' The prince paused. 'What I fear is the wrong itself, which might never be undone.'

The courtiers murmured.

'A great wrong?' the king said.

The prince held his shoulders back and looked directly at the king. 'Yes, Sire. A great wrong.'

'Which is?'

'I came across a maiden in the woods,' the prince said, 'and fell in love with her laughter.'

The courtiers tittered. Those near to Gwen and Lucy who recognised Lucy as the maiden whom the prince had found wandering in the woods gave her appraising looks. Lucy scowled at them.

'Go on,' King Ieldon said.

'I do not know what, by all the Beings, came over me. I only know I wished above all else to listen to her laughter all day long, and I ...' he hesitated and Gwen strained forward, anxious to hear what would come next '... bewitched the lady and brought her here to Ilatias.'

The courtiers gasped.

The king rose from his throne, descended to the green carpet and strode to the prince, so quickly that his royal cape of green silk threaded with real silver billowed behind him.

'You did what?'

Gwen shivered at the coldness in the king's voice.

Prince Elrane flinched. 'Sire, I am deeply ashamed.'

King Ieldon's black eyebrows rose. 'Her laugh? You bewitched a lady for her laugh?'

His eyes darkened with sorrow. 'You of all people, a prince of the realm, should know that to bewitch another living creature is contrary to every principle we hold dear. Only in the face of mortal danger is this allowed.'

'Yes.'

Prince Elrane faced the king squarely. 'I have deeply regretted my actions, right from the very day. I couldn't undo the enchantment and was too ashamed to seek help from the Seers.'

'Help you will have,' the king said in the same cold voice. 'First, however, I wish to know what your intolerable behaviour has to do with this case of trespass by the young man?'

The king turned to Mark who was staring open-mouthed at the prince.

'Do you mean my sister, Lucy? Is she the lady you're talking about? Did you enchant my sister?'

Gwen glanced at Lucy. Two bright spots of red blazed on Lucy's cheeks. She took a step forward, but Gwen clasped her wrist. 'Wait,' she said.

The king walked swiftly to Mark.

'Your sister?' he said.

'Yes,' the prince said. 'That is exactly what the two have to do with each other, Sire.'

He moved to stand beside Mark. 'I went to see the boy out of curiosity, to test the truthfulness of his claim to be Danae and his quest to see the king as the reason for his trespass.'

Another babble of excited chatter erupted at the mention of Danae. The king started, and scrutinised Mark as if he was some wonderful mythical beast.

The prince raised his voice over the chatter. 'I found the truth and more. I learned the Danae are not creatures from legend. And I learned the identity of the lady for whose laughter I had committed such wrongdoing.'

He cast around the rapt audience.

'The lady is the Lady Elizabeth,' the prince said, quietly, 'whom many of you know. She is really Lucy Godwin, a Danae, and sister to this young man who has battled the dangers of the Deep Forest of Arneithe in search of her.'

The courtiers murmured.

'Knowing this,' the prince said, 'I can no longer let my pride injure any chance of the lady being cured. I would bring her to you, Sire, to have the lady restored to her former self.'

Gwen reached for Lucy's hand.

King Ieldon returned to his throne with a heavy tread. He heaved a huge sigh, put his hands on his silk-clad knees and said, 'Is this lady here so we may speak with her?'

'Yes, Sire.'

Mark turned on his heel to search the room. His eyes lit on Lucy and Gwen as the prince said, 'Please be aware Sire, the lady does not know her former life or who she is. Be gentle in your questioning as she is softly spoken and easily confused.'

'Lucy!' Mark leaped across the room.

'Mark!' Lucy ran to meet him.

The courtiers' eyes widened.

The prince stared.

Lucy hugged Mark, pushed him away to laugh into his

freckled face, pulled him to her again and finally let him go. Mark danced about, grinning. Gwen ran across to them and all three hugged and laughed.

The chattering of the courtiers rose to new heights.

The king gave the queen a bemused look.

At last Lucy faced Prince Elrane. Her blue eyes flashed.

'The former Lady Elizabeth, Your Highness, has woken and is in her right mind,' she said, not at all softly. 'I am not confused. I know well who I am. As you say, I am Lucy Godwin, a Danae of the Forest, sister to Mark and to Gwen.'

The prince fell to his knees at Lucy's feet.

'My lady, can it be?' he said. 'You are recovered? You know who you are?' He lifted his handsome head to gaze into her eyes. 'Please! Can you find it in your heart to forgive me?'

The courtiers leaned forward as one, to see this spectacle more clearly. The queen covered her mouth with her hand. The king sat very upright and very still.

Lucy returned the prince's gaze, unsmiling.

'How?' the prince asked.

'By the same Sleih magic with which you enchanted me,' Lucy said, flushing palest pink.

King Ieldon once more left his throne.

'Lady,' he said to Lucy, 'our shame is deep at our son's wrongdoing, and this will not be the end of the matter because you, my lady, appear recovered. I would learn how this recovery was worked. However, that must wait.'

He frowned deeply at the kneeling prince. 'I still do not understand what this has to do with the charge of trespass.'

The prince stood and bowed to the king. 'Sire, I wish above all things to make amends, however small, for my conduct towards the lady. By helping her brother, I can begin to do so.'

The king nodded and the queen smiled. The courtiers buzzed their approval.

'Therefore,' Prince Elrane said, 'I am declaring Mark of the

Danae a friend to myself and to the House of Wood. As such he is always welcome in the King's Tower and cannot be guilty of trespass.'

The king stroked his smooth chin. 'The charge is dismissed,' he said gravely to Mark, 'on one condition.'

Chapter Thirty Five

A Plea Is Finally Made

'Condition?' Mark frowned.

'Yes,' King Ieldon said in the same grave tone. 'I would know the purpose of your trespass, as the prince suggests you are on a quest to seek an audience with us.'

Now? This was the moment they were finally able to make their plea to the king of the Sleih? Mark opened his mouth, glanced sideways at Gwen's anxious face, and shut his mouth. He bowed awkwardly.

'Your Majesty,' he said, 'once upon a time the Danae lived among the Sleih and the Madach but we were driven out because the Madach wanted our rich lands.'

Mark had the fleeting thought this story was different from the one Josh told, but it was the story he'd always known. Besides, the king's eyes had grown dark, as if the story might be something he had once heard too.

'Now Madach have come across the ocean,' Mark said. 'They're cutting down our trees and killing the wild creatures. Our people are scared we'll be driven out, like before. We haven't any weapons to defend ourselves.'

'What has happened to the people?' The queen's grasp on the arms of her throne tightened.

'Your Majesty,' Gwen said, 'my brother and I fled the village the day we were discovered. We don't know what's happening at home.'

Mark heard the sudden sob in Gwen's voice.

The queen wrung her hands in her lap. The courtiers drank in this new drama.

'So you require help of us?' King Ieldon said.

'Yes, Sire,' Gwen said. 'We believe the Sleih helped us once before against the Madach, and we hope you might help us this time too.'

The King's Secretary coughed politely. 'If I may venture my view, Sire,' he said, 'this must be the work of Rafe, Lord of Etting, whose ambitions are boundless. Arneithe is a vast Forest and will serve as an endless supply to build warships and as fuel for his manufactories. And once the Forest is razed, there may be minerals in the earth to be mined for making more weapons of war. He will not give it up lightly.'

A razed Forest, dug over for minerals? Mark's head hurt. What would happen to the Danae? And to the animals and birds Callie always worried about?

Lucy was white. Gwen had gone green, as if she might be sick.

The Secretary hadn't finished. 'Majesty, we should also consider the Danae themselves are of value to Lord Rafe, to sell in the slave markets. It is unlikely he will do them harm.'

Mark exchanged looks with Gwen and Lucy. Not much of a comfort.

The silence in the court deepened. Everyone waited for the king to speak.

***

It wasn't the king who spoke next.

Gwen's attention was taken by a lady stepping forward. Blue stones and white diamonds glittered in her dark braids as she paced with a determined step through the sunlight filling the room.

'Majesty, may I speak?' the lady said.

'Of course, Lady Melda.'

The lady's green gaze swept over Gwen, Mark and Lucy. Gwen didn't like the contempt she saw there.

'Majesty,' the lady said, bowing her head. 'The prince may not have acted as honourably as we would expect. However, he is a young man, and we do not know how much the so-called Lady Elizabeth tempted him to his actions.'

The lady was apparently heedless of Lucy's daggered glower.

'Whatever happened,' the lady said, 'it does not mean the Sleih should put themselves in mortal danger for the sake of a few villagers at the edge of the known world.'

Gwen clenched her fists.

The king arched his fine eyebrows.

'If this Rafe is indeed as ambitious as the Lord Secretary declares,' the lady said, 'we would be better defending Ilatias rather than sending our fighting men on a long and fruitless journey.' She favoured Gwen, Mark and Lucy with another cool glance. 'These children say they have been travelling for a long time. If what they say is true, it is possible there is now nothing in the Forest to defend.'

Mark gulped.

Lucy whispered, 'No, oh no.'

Prince Elrane looked at Lucy, although his words were for the king.

'Sire,' he said, 'in atonement for my wrongs, I personally will lead an army to drive Rafe's people into the sea. I will take Rafe on in his own land of Etting and defeat him utterly, before he can possibly think of heading our way.'

Gwen unclenched her fists. Lucy gave a slight nod.

'Mmm,' the king said, 'that's one plan. And thank you, Lady Melda, for your views.' He rose from his throne and offered his arm to the queen. 'We will leave you now, to think further on this with our Council, but be assured,' he said to Gwen, 'your plea will be considered with all seriousness.'

As the king and queen left the room, Gwen felt goosebumps

rising on her back. She turned her head, and caught the narrowed eyes of Lady Melda resting on her. The lady dropped her gaze and walked from the room.

Lucy, Mark and Gwen stood before the empty thrones.

Mark gave a skip. 'We did it, we did it. We reached the Sleih and we made our plea. And'–he grinned at Lucy–'we found Lucy. We can take Lucy home, like we promised Ma and Callie.'

Gwen grinned too. 'Yes, we did, and yes we can. Hopefully with the army of Sleih we also promised.' She puffed out a breath. 'I hope Lady Melda doesn't have too much to say about it. She doesn't like us, does she?'

Mark grunted a yes. He was watching Prince Elrane, standing alone, his eyes fixed on Lucy. Gwen watched too.

Prince Elrane approached, hesitantly. He kneeled before Lucy's upright figure.

'My lady,' he said, 'there is much for me to apologise for. I have shown little care in the past. I have been selfish and arrogant. I allowed my desire to rule my sense and my compassion. I placed my pride above your needs.'

Lucy widened her eyes slightly, encouraging the prince to go on with his confession.

'Now,' Prince Elrane said, 'I care greatly, that all should be well with you and your people.'

Mark's head jerked up. He glanced at Gwen, who whispered, 'Verian? Some will not care, but care they will?'

'I would be grateful,' Prince Elrane said to Lucy, 'if you would allow me to accompany you all back to your home.'

Lucy drew in a breath and held it.

Gwen narrowed her eyes. Her own view was that this request should not be easily granted. But she knew Lucy's forgiving ways. She knew too that Prince Elrane's defence of Mark would speak to Lucy far more than any apologies to herself.

'He's all right, honestly,' Mark murmured to Gwen. 'He was

kind to me.'

Gwen humphed. 'As he should have been.'

Lucy let out her breath and stretched her hands to the prince to encourage him to stand.

'I thank you for your apology, Prince,' she said. 'We would be pleased to have your company.'

Chapter Thirty Six

Conspiracy

'At least we know who they are, what they look like and where they're living,' Lady Melda said to the rat.

She paced her solar, her mind bustling like a village square on a festive day.

The rat was perched on the window sill chewing a mouldy bone. A long red gash glowed livid from its pointy nose to one beady eye.

'But how to stop old Ieldon from giving in to their pretty pleas? Hey?'

The rat stopped gnawing. *Easy. Pay a visit, cast all their minds into oblivion.*

Lady Melda threw the rat a thoughtful glance and went back to pacing.

'Tempting, tempting. Can't be done, though. Too late. They've seen the king. Too many people feel sorry for them. All made worse by their friendship with our spoilt brat of a prince.'

She stopped pacing, clasped her hands behind her and gazed up to the ornately painted ceiling. 'There's something else. The girl, what's her name, Gwen. A power hovers about her. Need to know where it comes from, what it is.'

The rat appeared less than interested.

Lady Melda stamped a blue-slippered foot. 'Those damnable Madach. Stupid, stupid.'

She absently stroked the rat's head. 'They *were* there, with the robbers, weren't they? So it's possible, even likely, they're in league with these robbers, eh ratty?'

The rat put its head on one side, as if pondering where this was going.

Discredit them? it suggested, and received a firmer than usual pat on the head in acknowledgement of its cleverness.

'Need to know more,' Lady Melda said. 'Need a few nuggets to throw into the pot, leave silly old Ieldon asking how he could have been taken in by 'Lady Golden Curls' and Miss 'Ooh, the Nasty Madach are Coming.''

She tickled the rat under the chin. 'And I know exactly the person to help us.'

The rat went back to its bone.

***

Coral examined the fresh fish, trying to decide what Lucy, Mark and Gwen would have for their supper. No doubt Prince Elrane would eat with them again. Coral liked having the prince around more. He was charming and generous. No matter the gossip about his behaviour towards the Lady Elizabeth (Coral couldn't get used to her being plain Lucy), Coral was sure it was one of those harmless things. After all, Lady Elizabeth/ Lucy was fine now. And having Gwen and Mark in the house had cheered the place up enormously, especially Mark, whose enthusiasm for everything new made Coral laugh every day.

Distracted by these thoughts, Coral at first didn't hear her name being called. When she did, she wondered why Lady Melda, one of the wisest and most powerful of the Sleih Seers, would be beckoning her. No one ignored a summons by a Seer, so Coral hurried to where the lady stood beside a tall gateway.

'Lady Melda, were you calling me?'

'Your name is Coral? Correct? And you are in the employ of the prince, working for the so-called Danae girl and her brother and sister? Correct?'

'Why, yes, my lady, I'm Coral.'

'Good. Come with me.'

Coral followed Lady Melda into a courtyard where stone urns spilled over with flowers in all shades of blue hanging delicately on silver stems. Blue-branched vines covered in glittering silver flowers and alive with blue and silver butterflies cascaded down the walls and fountains of silver water bubbled over blue stone sculptures of fantastical creatures.

Coral had no time to admire the pretty courtyard. She was hurried into a cool hallway and through to a reception room. Lady Melda seated herself on a blue chair and draped one arm over its silver-embroidered cushion.

'You are fond of our prince, are you not, Coral?'

'Of course, my lady. We all adore our young prince.'

'Exactly.' Lady Melda's sea-green eyes held Coral's gaze as she went on, unhurriedly. 'Can you see how these young Danae are taking advantage of him, using his good nature against him?'

Coral looked into Lady Melda's eyes, and understood she hadn't seen it at all. Not until now.

Lady Melda wagged a slim finger at Coral. 'I do believe they aren't Danae at all. A fairytale! What nonsense!'

Yes, nonsense. Coral saw that clearly.

'They're poor Madach village folk,' Lady Melda said, 'and this entire story about the Danae being in trouble is a sham.'

Of course. Lucy/Elizabeth had charmed her way into the prince's graces before sending for her brother and sister to come along as well. Now they were all living a comfortable life at the prince's expense. Poor Prince Elrane! It wasn't he who had bewitched the lady. It was the other way around.

'Would you like to help the prince, Coral? Help him see the truth?'

'Why, of course, my lady.' Coral was grateful someone as

important as Lady Melda had seen the truth and cared for the prince. 'What should I do, my lady?'

'I have a simple task for you. You will listen whenever possible to what these so-called Danae talk about and you will come to me each day to tell me what you have learned.'

Coral nodded enthusiastically. She didn't take her eyes off the lady's face.

'Do you think you can help me, Coral? For the prince's sake?'

'Why, of course, my lady.'

'Good, excellent. I will see you tomorrow.'

Lady Melda gazed into her lap. Coral, feeling as though she was coming out of a daydream, realised she'd been dismissed.

She curtsied. 'Thank you, my lady.'

A servant led her across the pretty blue and silver courtyard and through the gateway. Out in the street, Coral tapped her shopping basket against her side.

Poor Prince Elrane. Those wicked so-called Danae. Well, she, Coral, would help her prince. Thank the Beings Lady Melda cared what became of him.

Chapter Thirty Seven

Waiting

If Gwen expected an army of Sleih to march out of Ilatias the day after their audience with the king, she was disappointed.

King Ieldon invited Gwen and Lucy for lunch in a room of such magical beauty Gwen wished she could pick it up and take it home to her mother as a gift.

The rugs on the white and pink marble floor were patterned with bright birds which flew – really flew, albeit with slow deliberation – between trees with leaves truly shimmering in glittering sunlight. The yellow stone walls were draped with tapestries of picnics on mountain meadows where the picnickers slowly drank and ate and laughed amid wildflowers which trembled in a summer breeze; and big and small pictures showed green-gladed forests where deer leaped between silver-trunked trees and baby foxes tumbled among brilliant bluebells.

The doors of the room were flung open to a courtyard cooled by the silver spray of a mountain-shaped fountain, the mountain tipped with white marble and decorated with wolves, bears, lions and eagles carefully roaming its craggy sides.

Prince Elrane wasn't invited to the lunch. There were only the three of them. After the servants laid the food on silver plates, poured fresh juices into crystal glasses, inquired if anything else was needed and left with the footfalls of cats, King Ieldon asked Gwen and Lucy to tell him everything.

Lucy told what she remembered of the day she went picking wild garlic. Including about Callie.

'Your sister recalled nothing?' King Ieldon said.

'Nothing,' Gwen said.

'And her behaviour afterwards?'

Gwen laughed. 'As Mark always claims, Sire, Callie is strange in any case. Those awful nightmares,' she said to Lucy who nodded. 'Especially in the winter when the beast that haunts the Forest cried out in the night.'

King Ieldon cocked his head at the mention of the beast.

'But...' Gwen sipped at her juice before going on. 'Afterwards, Callie did seem more strange than normal. I know it's an odd thing to say, but I'm certain it was because of Callie that Mark and I happily accepted the idea of setting off on what was obviously a mad quest, and that Ma let us go.'

'Hmm.' King Ieldon sipped his golden apricot nectar, set down the goblet and turned to Lucy.

'Your recovery from my son's enchantment'–pain shadowed King Ieldon's face–'could have been effected, lady Lucy, by the Seers or by myself. The fact we weren't needed intrigues me. How was it done?'

'We think it was Gwen's pendant,' Lucy said.

Gwen untucked her tiny gryphon from its hiding place behind the collar of her red silk blouse. She showed it to King Ieldon.

'I gave it to Lucy to hold, she screamed and fainted and then she was Lucy again.'

King Ieldon peered at the tiny jewel for so long Gwen started to unclasp the chain, saying, 'Would you like to hold it, Sire?'

King Ieldon slowly shook his head. 'No, no. It is indeed a pretty piece, which must be imbued with magic. Enough to counteract Elrane's enchantment at least.' He laughed. 'My son's magic must not be as mature as we, or he, assume.

Perhaps we won't tell him how he has been bested by a jewel, even if it is a gryphon.'

'Are gryphons special, Sire?' Lucy said, smiling.

Gwen considered Lucy's smile strained. Perhaps she was mildly insulted to have been enchanted by weak magic. Gwen would have been insulted on Lucy's behalf, only she wasn't entirely certain the king was correct, or that he even meant what he said. Though why should that be ...?

'Oh, indeed yes,' King Ieldon said. He picked a grape from a bowl on the table, waved it in the air, and said, 'The Sleih and the gryphon have a long entwined history, a long history indeed.'

Again Gwen had the feeling King Ieldon was saying less than he could have. Her curiosity would have to wait. Her manners wouldn't allow her to ask a king for explanations.

No more was said about enchantments and gryphons. King Ieldon wanted to learn about the Danae and their history, and about the villages nestled against the ridge at the edge of the Forest beside the boundless oceans.

'I expect my Council to be swift in their decision,' he said, 'and then I myself will lead this venture to rescue the Danae, for I would see this Forest of yours with my own eyes.'

When the servants returned to clear the plates, Lucy and Gwen made their thanks and farewells. As they left the magical room, Gwen turned to the king.

'Sire,' she said. 'I forgot to say how the gryphon changed after it had done whatever it did for Lucy.'

'Changed?'

'Yes. It shifted so it was facing forwards, wings upraised and a tiny ruby tongue poking from a snarling mouth.'

King Ieldon's green eyes widened, and narrowed again so quickly Gwen wasn't certain she'd seen anything at all.

***

Days went by and the army of Sleih of Gwen's imaginings had yet to march from Ilatias. The King's Council met daily, and Gwen, Lucy and Mark expected news daily, but news did not come.

Patience was hard.

To make use of their enforced waiting, Prince Elrane encouraged Gwen and Mark to spend time each day at the King's School for Young Squires, where boys and girls of the Sleih learned about horsemanship and weaponry.

Mark was thrilled. At any time of the day, he could be found at the archery range, moving ever closer to his dream of a perfect score. Or he would be in the grassy practice square, cutting and thrusting his way through set sword drills.

The Master of the Squires declared Mark had talent and would one day make a fine soldier.

Lucy humphed and asked what their mother would have to say.

'Might be useful before this is over,' Mark said.

Lucy, too old for the School, practised under the tutelage of the prince's own masters. She decided she had little ability with weapons but stuck at it doggedly.

'I'd rather be on our way and trust to the real soldiers,' she said to Gwen. 'But if the king can't help us, we'll at least be better prepared to defend the villages ourselves.'

Gwen raised her eyebrows.

She herself discovered a talent for archery, and visions of the Madach invaders cowering under a shower of arrows as they fled back to their ships kept her firing at the straw targets for long hours. And then there was Beauty, one of the long-legged black horses popular with the Sleih lords and ladies and given to Gwen to learn to ride, as Mark and Lucy were also given their own black horses. Gwen loved the great beast and Beauty's noisy whinnying whenever Gwen came to her stable showed the feeling was mutual.

And still they waited for word from the king, and still none came.

One evening, Gwen, Mark, Lucy and Prince Elrane sat in Lucy's courtyard where the light from the few lamps flickered palely beneath the sparkling stars. A huge yellow moon squatted heavily above them.

They sat, brooding, restless.

Prince Elrane said, as if to lighten the mood, 'Your gryphon necklace, Gwen. I've been meaning to ask where it came from.'

Gwen touched the pendant which never left her throat. 'Josh, an old Danae Mark and I met in the Deep Forest, gave it to me. He said it belonged to his great-great many times Sleih grandmamma.'

'Sleih grandmamma? Hmm.' The prince eyed the tiny gryphon. 'You should be most careful with your jewel, Gwen. I suspect its value is beyond money.'

Coral was clearing the last of the plates. At the prince's words, she sneaked a glance at the pendant and left the courtyard looking more thoughtful than was necessary to carry dirty dishes.

***

More days passed. The night air grew too cool to sit in Lucy's courtyard in the evenings. The knot in Gwen's stomach tightened. Should they leave, or wait?

'Summer's over,' she said at supper one night. 'We have to go, with or without help, before winter arrives.'

'We should have gone already,' Lucy said.

Mark speared another potato with his fork and nodded.

'I agree.' Prince Elrane looked at Lucy. 'This waiting is dangerous. We have to make our own arrangements.'

'You'll come with us?' Mark said, swallowing potato.

'Yes.'

Gwen's distrust of Prince Elrane, already dulled in light of his willingness to beg his father daily to hasten the Council's decision, finally dissolved in a mist of gratitude.

It was as Verian had said, one who hadn't cared, now cared

deeply.

'Yes,' Prince Elrane said again. 'We will leave in two days.'

Chapter Thirty Eight

The King's Blessing

'You will understand,' King Ieldon said, 'it's not an easy decision to send fighting men to a far off place to defend a people of whom we know nothing. Indeed, whom most believe do not exist.'

Gwen sighed. She and Prince Elrane sat on green velvet stools before the king's desk in his study. The walls of the study were also draped in green velvet, with paintings of former kings and queens and of majestic black or blue-feathered gryphons, all of them against backdrops of ancient forest or snow-capped alps.

The gryphon and the Sleih did indeed have a long shared history. A startling thought came to Gwen.

Were the gryphons real?

No. The Sleih used them to pose with, as others, according to old fairytales, used unicorns or dragons.

She left thoughts of gryphons to concentrate on the king's excuses for the lack of any decision to help the Danae.

'Some on the Council argue we cannot know when or if this Lord Rafe might decide to attack the Citadel and we should be planning to defend ourselves rather than running off to the end of the world.'

'There is no reason Rafe would attack us, Sire,' Prince Elrane said. 'He has much to do still in the Forest, and in Arneithe, and numerous countries to conquer closer to home before reaching the Kingdom.'

The king pushed back his long hair and sighed. 'I agree, son. Others do not.' He looked at Gwen. 'I need something to make them believe. I need proof you, lady Gwen, and your brother and sister are truly Danae, not, as some are saying, poor Madach village folk seeking fame and fortune.'

Gwen grew hot, then very cold. Would they really have to leave, simply the four of them, and hope to rescue the villagers themselves? Would it be enough to return with one prince and new skills with swords and bows?

She and Mark, and Lucy, had been through too much for such a paltry return, surely?

'I don't know what I can say to help, Sire,' she said. Tears welled, and without thinking, Gwen blurted, 'It's what Josh warned us, about the Sleih. Not much help before, was what he said, and what help they did give, they demanded a high price for it.' She stopped, blushing, absently fingering her pendant. 'I'm sorry ...'

'No, don't be sorry,' the king said. His eyes, fixed on the silver gryphon, were black.

'A gryphon. Yes, of course,' he said at last. 'And also ...' he looked at Gwen. 'Did you say Josh talked about a high price for our help? Did he know what that price was?'

The way the king asked the question suggested to Gwen he knew the answer. Was this a test?

Gwen lifted her shoulders and returned the king's gaze. 'Yes, Sire. The Sleih kept behind the youngest child from each family.' She paused. 'Josh's baby sister, Clara, was one of them.'

The king's head sunk to his chest. 'Yes,' he said quietly, 'Clara was one of them.'

'Father?' Prince Elrane stood up and took a step closer to the desk. 'Is this true?'

The king lifted his head. 'Yes. It's true.' He sighed deeply. 'Thank you, Gwen. I have been foolish thinking the Council would grant your cry for help out of the goodness of their hearts. Now I see I must bring to light old wrongs and frighten them with old prophecies to make them see sense.'

Gwen had no idea what this speech meant. The king smiled and she smiled back, while Prince Elrane said, all in a rush, 'Does this mean I have your blessing, Sire, to set out immediately with a handful of men, and if the Council does finally agree, a larger force may follow?'

'Yes,' the king said. 'Go with my blessing. I will deal with the Council. But I do not think a large force will be needed, do you Gwen?'

This new conversation had Gwen floundering. 'Umm ...'

'There are only sailors and woodsmen and perhaps a few soldiers, isn't that so?'

'Oh, yes. An army's probably not needed.' Gwen let go her glorious vision. 'Enough soldiers on black horses with shining swords to scare them back to Etting.'

'On black horses ...' The king glanced at Prince Elrane. 'They have their own?'

'Yes, Sire.'

'The horses ...?'

'We have not yet reached there Sire.' He raised his eyes to the ornate ceiling. 'How stupid of me!'

'Test them today and send word to me at the Council.'

Gwen's confusion was complete, although her heart was less heavy.

Chapter Thirty Nine

Tests, Truths And Prophecies

Prince Elrane led Lucy, Mark and Gwen down the busy, cobbled winding road and out through the crowds jostling to make their way through the gates.

The four of them rode their tall black horses.

The heat of the day had passed and the cool breezes of an early autumn evening refreshed the air. The sky was clear. The party trotted steadily along the road, weaving between the many pedestrians, carts, carriages and other riders, until Prince Elrane turned onto an empty track. Here he urged his horse to a canter.

Mark rode beside Prince Elrane at the front. Gwen, following with Lucy, let herself enjoy the ride, loving Beauty's fluid movement.

She sensed a growing excitement in the horse.

'What's going on, Beauty?' she said.

Beauty shook her shining mane.

Prince Elrane jumped his horse over a gate into a freshly mown field and stopped, watching Gwen, Mark and Lucy each take the gate and line up before him.

'This is normally the last part of the formal training of the squires of the Sleih,' the prince said. His sea green eyes glinted in the evening light. 'But we must bring it forward for you, and for different reasons than training.'

Gwen waited for the different reasons, but Prince Elrane

only said, 'I need you to gallop across the field after me. You'll hear me shout out a command. Do nothing, only hold tight.'

Gwen exchanged a frown with Mark. There was a tension in the prince's voice which brought about a tiny thudding, a hint of anxiety, inside her.

'What's going on?' she whispered to Lucy.

Lucy gave a tiny smile. 'You'll see,' she said.

Gwen leaned towards Mark, but his hazel eyes were fixed on Prince Elrane who had wheeled his horse around and was galloping across the field.

Gwen had no need to spur Beauty to follow. Beauty tossed her mane, whinnied her excitement, and galloped after the prince's horse.

Prince Elrane shouted, 'Fly!'

***

'Your Majesty, and fellow councillors, I have news which will cause us all to think twice about heeding the request of these so-called Danae children.'

Ieldon groaned inwardly. His early expectation that his Council would quickly decide to go to the aid of the Danae – who were, as the stories said, their own kin – had been frustrated by Lady Melda. She had sowed such doubt that the arguments had gone back and forth for days.

'I am convinced these young people are not who they say they are.' Lady Melda favoured her fellow councillors with a mildly outraged glare. 'I believe they are in league with robber Madach, and possibly belong to a robber gang.'

The councillors murmured.

'It has come to light,' Lady Melda said, 'these Danae are in possession of a priceless jewel, stolen from an old man living in the woods. A poor old man who couldn't judge its value.'

Lady Melda's outraged glare strengthened.

'And I also know these children were with robber Madach a short time before their arrival in the Citadel.'

Ieldon was puzzled as to why Lady Melda ground her teeth.

'It causes me to discount the truth of the boy's story,' she said, 'of trespassing in the Tower grounds because he must deliver his plea to you, Majesty.'

Ieldon averted his eyes from Lady Melda's righteous gaze, but she hadn't finished.

'More likely, he was intent on theft. I do not think such as these are deserving of our assistance. Do you, Your Majesty?'

Ieldon shifted in his chair, fidgeting with the papers in front of him. Why was Melda being difficult about this? He glanced at her stern face. No, he assured himself, it was because she cared so much. Lady Melda could always be counted on for caring strongly that the Council should make the right decision.

No matter how long it took.

The other councillors whispered to each other. One, who had previously wanted to help the Danae, spoke out.

'This is indeed worrying, Majesty. Have we been too hasty in accepting their story?'

Ieldon stopped fidgeting. He surveyed his councillors.

'We will end this indecision,' he said. 'But to do so, you force me to break a sacred oath.' He looked at Lady Melda. 'I do not believe the young Danae stole, nor that they are in league with robber Madach. Their story rings true to me.'

He abruptly rose and walked to the door. 'I will show you why,' he said, opening the door.

Ieldon beckoned to the Seer waiting in the hallway. A messenger also waited. He handed Ieldon a rolled-up note which Ieldon slipped, unread, onto the table as he retook his seat.

'Councillors,' Ieldon said, 'you know Lady Clara, respected Healer and Seer of our Sleih kingdom.'

Clara smiled a greeting and the councillors nodded, their respect for the Seer apparent. She was a little taller and a little broader than most Sleih, and while Ieldon knew her years numbered a great many, they showed gently on her. There were few grey streaks in her thick black hair, held in a bun at the nape of her neck, and the lines around her kindly sea-green eyes were lightly etched.

'Lady Clara,' Ieldon said, 'will you please tell this Council what I told you, in confidence, several days ago?'

'Your Majesty told me,' Clara said, 'I am not a full-blooded Sleih as I was brought up to believe. I am, in truth, of the Danae.'

Ieldon enjoyed the oohs and aahs around the table.

'Your Majesty told me,' Clara said, 'of your grandfather's reluctance to force the Danae from the kingdom, knowing they were being sent to face the dangers of Arneithe.'

'And?' Ieldon said.

Clara spoke slowly. 'He asked each Danae family if they would leave behind one child, very young and with the look of the Sleih. The child would be raised as a Sleih lord or lady. No one would know they were Danae, including themselves.'

Clara paused. When she spoke next, her voice was low. 'Many families gave a child, reluctantly, knowing as the king did that the days ahead would be difficult and dangerous and the Danae might not survive. I am one of those children.'

The councillors murmured.

Lady Melda frowned and touched the tips of her fingers together. 'Why did we not know of this?' she said.

'My grandfather swore all who were there,' Ieldon said, 'all who took these Danae babes into their homes, to eternal secrecy. A sacred vow – one you have forced me to break.'

Ieldon gazed at his silent councillors. 'Many are gone from us, of course. It has indeed been a long time since these events. However, as a Seer exercising her Sleih powers to the fullest, Lady Clara has been privileged with a long life.'

He looked from face to face around the table. 'Once, the Madach and the Sleih of this land did the Danae an appalling wrong, forcing them to leave their homes, forcing them to give up their children. Madach are once again persecuting the Danae – the Danae whom, all of you should bear in mind, are of our blood.'

Ieldon had his Council's full attention.

'We owe a debt of honour to these people and that alone should make your decision easy. However, there is one more thing.'

The king let the silence grow. He lifted his head and spoke loudly, an actor reciting his lines:

'There will come a time when the Danae will play a great role in the future of the Kingdom. Without the Danae, there will come a time when there is no Kingdom, not one such as we know now, or in days past.'

The silence stayed.

Ieldon broke it. 'It is a prophecy, by the Lord Gryphon who counselled my grandfather at the time the Danae were forced into exile. It was part of the reason he took the step of asking families to give up a child, so a Danae presence would remain in the Kingdom. A sort of insurance.'

Ieldon sighed. 'While I have no idea what this prophecy portends, it's clear to me our obligation is not only to the Danae. It is also to ourselves.'

The silence deepened. Ieldon waited, and wasn't disappointed.

'This is all very good, Sire,' Lady Melda said. 'And would persuade even me to this cause.'

Possibly only Ieldon heard her restrained contempt.

'However,' Lady Melda's voice trembled – with anger? 'We only have these children's word that they are indeed Danae. I very much doubt the truth of their claim given what I have learned and told this Council. I maintain they are simply Madach trash, thieves and liars.'

Her words set the councillors to more murmurs and

whispers and head nodding and shaking, during which Ieldon reached for and unrolled the note on the table. He scanned it and drew a deep, grateful breath. He held a hand up for quiet.

'I beg to differ, Lady Melda,' he said. He smoothed the note with his hand and smiled at her. 'I have just received word.'

Ieldon shifted his smile to take in the whole Council, ensuring each would hear his words.

'The horses obey them,' he said.

He waited a beat to let the councillors take this in before adding, 'And we know, all of us know, don't we, the horses only obey those with Sleih blood, never for the Madach, trash or otherwise.'

An image of Gwen's silver pendant filled Ieldon's mind.

'Or perhaps,' he said, 'they obey only those with gryphon magic in their souls, no matter how deep the magic lies.'

Chapter Forty

Lord Rafe Has News

In far off Etting, Lord Rafe rested his hands on the parapet of the tallest tower of his castle. The views were wide and far, and all he could see belonged to him. As did lands over the horizon to the west and to the south and to the east.

And, he hoped, lands over the horizon to the north, although he would only know for certain when his expedition returned. His black eyes gleamed at the vision of the two ships sat heavily in the sea, laden with valuable cargo of timber, and fairytale folk.

The view before him was of early autumn. The apple orchards close by the castle walls were heavy with fruit, the plums and cherries having already given up their harvest. Reds and oranges dotted the mature green of the woods beyond. Further in the distance, the fields were a patchwork of cleared brown earth and waving gold where farmers laboured to bring in their crops.

Rafe saw none of this. His mind's eye was far beyond the view. He was thinking about the visit of Lady Melda. Had she been successful in stopping the Sleih sending help to the Danae? She had said she would send him a message. There had been no message.

Afterwards, Rafe considered it must have been because he was thinking of Lady Melda that he could suddenly hear her voice. She was talking quickly and clearly. He peered all around, as if he would find her there with him on the tower.

The voice went on, in his head.

Rafe, I know you can hear me. Listen, listen carefully. Over this great distance, I don't know how long I can hold our minds together, so listen.

She sounded angry.

I have delayed the rescue of the Danae, not stopped it. It may be enough. I will seek out your Captain Jarrow, and if the Danae remain free in their villages I will ensure such is not the case by the time the Sleih arrive.

Delayed, not stopped?

I will need a sign for Jarrow, to assure him I work with you on this. What should the sign be?

Rafe thought quickly. A sign for Jarrow. What could he give her?

Of course, Tristan. Here was Tristan's chance to redeem himself, prove he was a good son and a worthy heir after all. He spoke out loud into the evening air.

'My lady, do not go to Jarrow. My own son, Tristan, is part of the expedition. Go to Tristan and tell him you and I are partners in building the empire which he will one day inherit. Remind him of the day he and I spoke on the ship, not long before the expedition left. Tell him I regret my manner with him that day. Tell him I know he is a good son and a worthy heir. Tell him I command him, no, I ask him, to do whatever you require of him to ensure the success of the expedition.'

He waited to hear her response, but there was only the calling of birds heading home for the night.

End of Book Two

If you have enjoyed this book, please leave a review on Amazon.

Guardians Of The Forest Book 3

Gryphon Magic

Chapter One

Captain Jarrow's Problems

Thwack!

The Madach woodsman hefted the axe high for another blow. The slim larch would soon fall.

Callie wriggled further around the beech, choking back a cough. Wood smoke from the piles of smouldering brush seared her throat.

'Don't see me, don't see me,' she whispered.

Other woodsmen waited to haul the felled tree onto the wagon. The horses, harnessed for the journey back to the ships, stood by patiently.

Callie knew these horses. They'd been taken from the Danae farmers early in the summer to do the jobs the Madach's monstrous machines should have done.

The nearest horse turned its head towards Callie and snickered quietly.

'Good horse,' Callie said softly. She nodded and the horse lowered its head.

One of the woodsmen, perhaps alerted by the horse, squinted in Callie's direction. He nudged his colleague.

'Nothing there,' the man said.

'You can't see me, you can't see me.' Callie slowly withdrew behind the beech.

Thwack!

The axeman jumped back from the larch. 'There it goes!'

'Go!' Callie hissed.

Four grown boar galloped from the beech wood. Their grunts filled the air. They tossed their massive heads, waved their giant tusks and charged the Madach as if they would impale them and throw them high into what remained of the trees.

The woodsmen screamed.

***

'What's going on!'

Tristan looked up from his place at the ship's railing at Captain Jarrow's bellow. The sweating faces of the woodsmen stumbling across the earth-packed wharf were white under their weathered tans – a stark contrast to Jarrow's livid red cheeks.

What had the wild creatures done now? Tristan held back a grin. He felt a tinge of sympathy for the men, given Jarrow's volatile temper seemed at bursting point this hot afternoon. No doubt he suffered deeply from the lack of sleep which afflicted all the Madach through the warm summer nights. The constant hooting of the owls perched in the ships' riggings and the need to keep doors and portholes closed against rampaging squirrels meant long, stuffy, uncomfortable nights for everyone on the ships.

The woodsmen huddled in a tight group, hanging grimly to the leads of the sturdy horses. They peered constantly over their shoulders, back up the rough track to the forest beyond.

'Why aren't you out there cutting down trees?' Jarrow's roar sent woodsmen and horses stumbling backwards.

Shuffling feet met his question, until the leader of the group said, gruffly, 'Boar, Captain.'

The others joined in.

'Huge boar, Capt'n, sir. Tusks like elephants!'

'Came chargin' us, out of nowhere.'

'Like before, 'cept more of 'em.'

219

Dark silence from Jarrow.

The woodsmen's leader tried to catch Jarrow's eye, perhaps hoping for a shard of compassion. Whatever the fellow saw made him glance away.

'Sorry, Capt'n,' he said. 'It's bad enough having to do all the work by hand, without having wild animals always at us.'

'Are you babies?' Jarrow thrust his ginger beard into the leader's face. 'By the Beings, they're pigs, they're not going to eat you.'

The woodsmen grimaced, uncertain about this.

Jarrow waved his hands. 'Bunch of babies, all of you. Get out of my sight.'

Scarlet-faced, the woodsmen quickly led the horses across the wharf to the newly built stables. The horses trotted along, eager for their dinners.

Jarrow squinted after them. His colourless gaze fell on Tristan. Tristan straightened up, nodded.

'Those damnable pigs,' Jarrow said. 'Bad enough they destroyed your father's expensive machines. Now they're attacking our workers.' His frizzy ginger hair fell across his forehead. 'Love to lock 'em up with that rebel Danae who helped 'em. Even better, hunt 'em down and feast on roast boar.'

Tristan made a note not to repeat this to Callie. So far, the boar had proven impossible to catch or kill and the attacks were becoming more frequent. It made the men reluctant to go into the forest and slowed the work of harvesting the timbers.

Which was the whole point as far as Tristan, Callie and the forest creatures were concerned.

Jarrow clenched his fists and Tristan read the man's frustration in his pinched lips and drawn eyebrows. He suspected that once more, at the dinner table, he and the lieutenants would have to listen to Jarrow's theory about the wild creatures being in league with the Danae on the night the machines were destroyed.

'Tame pigs!' Jarrow would say.

And when his lieutenants, and Tristan, frowned their scepticism, Jarrow would point out, quietly, how the troublesome squirrels never made their messes in the small cabin where the Danae senior Elder, Tomas, and the rebel, Peter, were held captive. Suspicious, hey? And they would murmur their agreement.

Jarrow rocked on his heels and barked a short laugh. 'Not long now before we have those Danae villagers out of this cursed forest and into the holds on their way to the slave markets. We'll be making our way back home to Etting and your noble father in no time at all, Sir Tristan.'

Tristan forced a smile.

'How can the animals help them then, hey, Sir Tristan? Hey?'

Jarrow's bad mood evaporated.

***

In the blackest hours of the night, Callie tossed on her bed of leaves under the sheltering branches of the willow. Her tousled dark curls were damp, her skin hot and clammy. She cried out, 'No, no!'

She runs and runs, breathless, towards the Danae at the edge of the Forest, trussed like lambs, hands and ankles tied.

She tries to call, 'I'm here, I'll free you.'

Her words are drowned by the market sellers' calls. 'A fairytale come to life, my lords and ladies, a fairytale!'

The rabbit, used to this restlessness, nestled in more closely. Callie woke, felt the soft fur close beside her and breathed in deeply. The dream dulled, the rabbit twitched, and Callie, hesitant to return to sleep, tried instead to think about what more she and the forest creatures could do to make life difficult for the Madach.

She wondered, sleepily, how the badgers were going with

their tunnelling under the wharf.

***

Tristan arrived not long after the sun rose, bringing Callie breakfast from the ship. The rabbit was off seeing to its own breakfast. Summer was moving on and an autumn chill hung in the air, dampening the willow's fading leaves.

Tristan was unusually silent.

'Is something wrong?' Callie said, her mouth full of bread and cheese.

Tristan shifted his back against the tree's bark. 'I think it's all about to get worse.'

'Worse?'

'Remember how you suggested the mice should spoil the food in the ships' stores?'

'And avoid any traps.'

'Oh, they've avoided the traps, and Jarrow's in a foul temper over the damage. He's figuring where he can get more food.'

Callie stared at him.

'No.'

***

Go to my website cherylburman.com to find out what inspired *The Guardians Of The Forest*. You can also buy Book One *The Wild Army* and Book Three *Gryphon Magic* from there or direct from Amazon.com or Amazon.co.uk in both kindle and paperback versions.

Printed in Great Britain
by Amazon

81034845R00127